THE STORYTELLER LIBRARY

A CHILD'S
TREASURY OF TALES

Retold by Lesley Young

SMITHMARK

To Josie Ainscough and Laurence Ainscough

This edition first published in 1996 by
Smithmark Publishers Inc.,
a division of US Media Holdings Inc.,
16 East 32nd Street, New York, NY 10016

Smithmark books are available for bulk purchase for sales promotion
and for premium use. For details, write or call the Manager of Special Sales,
Smithmark Publishers Inc, 16 East 32nd Street, New York, NY 10016;
(212) 532 6600

Produced by
Anness Publishing Limited
1 Boundary Row
London SE1 8HP

The Storyteller tales in this compendium were previously published
as individual titles.

ISBN 0 7651 9779 0

Printed and bound in China

2 4 6 8 10 9 7 5 3 1

CONTENTS

Cinderella

There was once a beautiful girl with golden hair and eyes as blue as the sky. She was very happy, until her mother became ill and died. Her father married again, but soon he died, too, and she was left with her stepmother and her two stepsisters.

They were very ugly, bad-tempered girls, and they were so jealous of her beauty that they made her wear an old grey dress and wooden shoes.

"It's your job to scrub the house, clean out the fire and cook," they told her.

She had to get up very early to fetch water from the well, and she spent all day on her hands and knees scrubbing, or making the meals.

"Ugh! We don't like this stew!"

"It's disgusting!" shouted her stepsisters, as they gobbled down the meals she made.

No matter what she did, it was never good enough.

"Have you turned my mattress? There's a lump in it," said one. "Go and do it now!"

"That's nothing! I found a feather in my pigeon pie!" said the other.

They made their stepsister wash and iron their fine dresses and the ribbons in their hair. But even in her old grey dress, her eyes shone out like the blue sky and she made them look uglier than ever.

At the end of a hard day, the girl had no warm bath to soak in or soft bed to sleep in. The poor girl used to huddle down beside the warm cinders of the fire, so she became known as Cinderella.

One morning, Cinderella carried through a steaming pile of toast, trying hard not to drop it. The two stepsisters were sitting at the table waving large white cards with gold crowns on them, and they were pink with excitement.

"There's a Grand Ball at the palace – and we're invited."

"The King has decided it's time for his son, the Prince, to choose a bride," said their mother. "He's asked all the girls in the land to the ball, so that he may choose one to be his wife."

"Am I invited then?" asked Cinderella.

"You?" screeched her stepmother, "in your rags, with smuts on your face?" and they all laughed so much that Cinderella rushed back to the kitchen and sobbed beside the fire.

Soon the night of the ball came.

"Pull tighter!" said her stepsisters, as she laced them into their silk ball gowns. She curled their hair with iron tongs, heated in the fire.

"Don't burn it!" they cried, "You're not making pastry now!" At last they were painted and powdered and covered in perfume. Cinderella couldn't help sneezing.

"Stop that!" they shouted. "You're only sneezing because you're jealous. Go and see if our carriage is there yet, and make us a snack for the journey."

Their mother appeared wearing bright blue silk, with feathers in her hair, looking like a plump, red-faced peacock. Then they all swept off in their carriage and, after all the hurry and fuss, Cinderella was quite alone.

She cleared up the powder and perfume and went back to the kitchen, but she was too sad to eat her scraps of bread and cheese. She opened the door and threw the bread out for the birds, as she did every night.

There was already a pale, watery moon in the sky. As she stood looking up at it, Cinderella wished with all her heart that she, too, could go to the ball.

Cinderella went back inside and sat down beside the kitchen fire and, as she thought about the grand ballroom and the handsome prince, a tear fell and sizzled on the grate.

"Why are you crying?" asked a gentle voice behind her. "And what are you doing here when you should be at the ball?"

Cinderella looked round and blinked. A little old lady in a red cloak stood there, with a round smiling face and a wand which sparkled at the tip like a firefly.

"How can I go to the ball," said Cinderella, "in these rags? How can I dance in these heavy wooden shoes? You don't know how much I long to dance!"

"Oh yes I do," said the old lady. "I am your fairy godmother," and she tapped Cinderella on the shoulder with the wand. At once Cinderella's rags vanished, and she was wearing a white silk ball gown that glittered with diamonds.

She twirled round and the silk swished and rustled, leaving a trail of perfume that was so gentle that it almost wasn't there. It smelled like summer rain.

Cinderella's feet felt as light as air, and when she looked down she saw beautiful glass slippers, twinkling in the firelight.

"Now you will go to the ball," said the fairy godmother.

"But there is no carriage to take me," said Cinderella.

The old lady looked round the kitchen. She picked up an apple and looked at it carefully. "No . . . Wait a minute, do you see that big pumpkin?" she said, pointing to the vegetable basket. "Help me carry it out into the garden."

She tapped it with her wand and, as Cinderella stared, it changed before her eyes into a glass coach that sparkled like ice. But what use was a glass coach with no horses?

Six fieldmice crouched nearby, dazzled by the shiny coach. The old lady tapped them lightly on their ears. They disappeared and in their place stood six white horses, tossing their manes in the night air.

"You need footmen – one to drive, and one to ride behind and make sure you arrive safely," said the old lady. She lifted a large leaf with her wand, and two frogs peeped out. When she tapped them with the wand, they vanished to be replaced by two footmen with white wigs and bulging eyes.

"Look after your mistress," she said.

"We will," they croaked.

"Now, off you go the the ball," said the fairy godmother. "But listen carefully and don't ever forget this – you must leave the palace before midnight. At the last stroke of Twelve, all your fine clothes will disappear and you will be back in your old grey rags." Cinderella promised, and thanked her with tears in her eyes, as she climbed into the coach.

"Oh, thank you again!" she shouted through the window, as the glass coach swept off in a cloud of dust.

At the palace, the ballroom blazed with the light from hundreds of candles. When Cinderella appeared at the top of the staircase, everyone stopped dancing and stared at her, wondering who the beautiful young stranger was. The band stopped playing and the Prince looked round to see what was happening.

"I think she must be a foreign princess," sniffed one of her stepsisters, never dreaming that this was Cinderella.

The Prince at once ran up the stairs, took her hands in his, and asked her to dance. As the music struck up again, and she was swept off in his arms, Cinderella felt that all her dreams had come true.

She had never learned to dance, but the glass slippers seemed to make it very easy and she felt as if she was floating on air. All evening, the Prince danced only with her. When others came up to ask her to dance, he held her hands tightly in his own and said, "No. This is my partner."

The Prince took her in to supper, and she ate a water ice that tasted like violets. At another table, she could see her stepsisters quarrelling over the last cherry in a bowl of ice cream. As she watched, her stepmother reached over and ate it herself. But Cinderella was too excited to eat much.

The Prince led her off again into the music. As they danced, he leaned down and said, "Did you know that your eyes are just like the sky?"

When he whispered in her ear, "Will you be my princess?" Cinderella felt she could dance with him for ever. But then she was startled by a loud noise like a gong.

"What's that?"

"Don't worry," laughed the Prince, "it's only the palace clock striking midnight, although it seems only seconds since we met."

"Midnight!" cried Cinderella, and she broke away from him and rushed out of the ballroom.

The guests drew back on either side to let her through, and the Prince ran after her, but she raced like the wind down the steps.

"Quick!" shouted the Prince. "Find her!"

Footmen ran off in all directions, looking for her, but she had vanished into the night.

In fact, Cinderella had climbed into the palace dovecot to hide. The doves knew that she was kind and fed birds in the cold weather, and they didn't make a noise. They sat at the entrance, spreading their feathers and hiding Cinderella, and the footmen ran past and never thought to look inside.

At last Cinderella was able to climb down and run home, wearing her old grey dress again.

But back at the palace, the Prince was holding something that sparkled in the moonlight. Cinderella had been in such a hurry that one of her glass slippers had fallen off and been left behind on the palace steps.

The Prince held it up. "I have found my princess," he said. "She is the owner of this slipper."

When her stepmother arrived back from the ball with her stepsisters, Cinderella was sitting in her old grey dress at her usual place beside the fire.

"Quick! Undo our laces!" screeched the sisters, throwing themselves into chairs and easing off their shoes to rub their feet.

"Bring me some tea!" said her stepmother, taking pins out of her hair. "So many people wanted to dance with us, we didn't have time to eat. What a ball! Isn't it a shame you'll never see such a thing? You can't imagine the dresses. And the jewels!"

"Isn't the Prince wonderful to dance with?" said one of the sisters.

"Oh, divine!" said the other, winking.

"And there was a mysterious foreign princess," said their mother, pouring her tea into her saucer. "It's so exciting – just like a fairy tale."

The Prince carried the glass slipper with him everywhere. He couldn't sleep, and said he would not rest until he had found his princess again. Then he had an idea and he sent for two of his best footmen.

"I want you to take this slipper and travel all over the land," he told them, "making sure that every girl in the country tries it on. I don't want to see you again until you have found the girl whose foot it fits."

For six days the footmen rushed all over the country, to grand houses, farms and cottages.

Every girl tried to make the slipper fit her. The girl in the dairy stopped churning butter and rubbed some on her foot, to try and make it slip inside. Grand ladies soaked their feet in hot perfumed water to see if they would shrink.

On the seventh day, the footmen arrived at Cinderella's house. Her stepsisters rushed to try on the glass slipper.

"I wondered where I'd lost that!" said one.

"Don't be silly, you know it's mine," said the other.

They huffed and puffed and screwed up their toes, but it was no use. They couldn't jam their feet into the dainty slipper.

"Is there no one else in the house?" asked the footmen.

"Only Cinderella," snorted the stepmother. "But she's just a servant, and she certainly doesn't go to balls."

"The Prince said that every girl must try it on," said the footmen. "Let her try."

The sisters went into the kitchen, where Cinderella was peeling a huge mound of potatoes.

"You're wanted in the drawing-room," they said, "but don't bother to wash, you'll be back peeling potatoes in a minute."

Cinderella went through, and a footman held out the glass slipper. She slipped her foot into it, and it fitted as if it had been made for her. Behind her, the ugly sisters gasped as she reached into a pocket in her old grey dress and pulled out the other glass slipper. It matched perfectly.

"There must be some mistake," spluttered her stepmother.

"There is no mistake," said the footmen. "This is our new princess – look how beautiful she is, with eyes like the sky." They took off their hats and bowed in front of Cinderella.

"We have a gold coach outside," said one. "Will you come with us now to the palace?"

Cinderella was still holding the potato knife. She handed it to one of her stepsisters, who took it as if it were a rose, and curtseyed.

"Can we come, too?" they squealed, "We are her sisters."

The footmen placed a cloak of sky blue silk over Cinderella's shoulders and said, "Hurry. The Prince is waiting."

The stepsisters and their mother were left in the courtyard, their mouths hanging open, as Cinderella went off in her golden coach.

The Prince stood at the top of the Palace steps and held out his arms in welcome. Cinderella ran up the steps, and the doves flew beside her, holding up her cloak.

"At last I have found my Princess," said the Prince, holding her to him, "and I'm never going to let you go this time."

More invitations were sent out, this time to a royal wedding.

In Cinderella's old home, her stepsisters had to make their own breakfast. "How can I make toast when you've let the fire go out?" snapped one.

"Oh, do it yourself," said the other. "It's all your fault. If we'd been nicer to Cinderella, we would have been asked to the wedding."

But then there was a knock at the door, and there stood a footman with a stiff white envelope. The stepsisters tore it open and found invitations to the royal wedding inside. Cinderella was so happy that she couldn't bear the thought of anyone being unhappy – even the stepsisters who had been so unkind to her.

The palace cook made twenty different kinds of
ice cream, and baked a cake that was big enough
for everyone in the country to have a slice.

On the morning of the wedding, the ballroom
was filled with so many white lilies and rose
trees, that it looked like a garden.

At the wedding party, the Prince held Cinderella tightly and said, "You're not going to disappear at midnight again, are you?"

"Never," replied Cinderella, and she went to the top of the staircase and looked through the crowd until she spotted her stepsisters, clinging to each other sadly in a corner.

Then she took her wedding bouquet of white roses and threw it down at them. They stretched up, caught it, and for a moment they didn't look ugly at all.

Turning back to the Prince, Cinderella smiled and said, "Wouldn't it be lovely if everyone could live happily ever after – just like us?"

A Storyteller Book

Beauty and the Beast

There was once a very rich merchant, who lived in a huge, grand house with his three daughters. They were all very pretty, but the youngest daughter was the prettiest. She was always smiling, showing two dimples in her creamy skin, and her smile was so lovely she became known as Beauty.

Her sisters sprawled about all day on silk couches, admiring themselves in mirrors, but Beauty had better things to do. She spent a lot of time visiting the old, poor people in the cottages nearby, and cheering them up.

Lots of young men wanted to marry the sisters. The two oldest always refused because they were waiting for a duke or a prince. However, Beauty always thanked the young men, but said she was too young to marry.

"Also," she explained with a smile, "I want to stay at home and look after Father when he's old."

One day at breakfast, a servant brought in a letter on a silver tray. The girls' father read it and went as white as the tablecloth.

"All my ships have been lost in a storm at sea. We are as poor as church mice now, so we must move to a small cottage and find what work we can."

"Work?" snapped the oldest sister in horror, while the middle sister piled even more strawberry jam on her bread, in case she couldn't have any more for a while.

"Don't worry, Father," said Beauty, going around to him and patting his forehead, "we'll be all right as long as we're all together."

"Let's go to a ball tonight. Perhaps we can find a couple of rich men to marry us," said Beauty's sisters.

But now that they were poor, no one wanted to marry them.

"Where is Beauty? We would marry her tomorrow, because she would be sure to make us happy," all the young men said.

The sisters were furious to hear this, and scowled so much that they looked quite cross and ugly.

After a short time the merchant and his daughters had to move out of their grand house. They all went to live in a tiny cottage in the heart of the countryside. When they moved in, it was damp and unwelcoming. The two elder sisters hated their new home, and did nothing but complain bitterly.

"How can we be expected to live in a place like this?" they moaned, huddling together beside a smoking fire.

Beauty, however, tied on an apron and set to work. She painted the rooms and put flowers everywhere. She smiled so kindly at the woodcutter who lived down the lane, that he left bundles of wood for her. Soon she had good fires going in all the rooms, and the cottage was filled with the smell of baking bread. While she worked, she sang, and she still managed to find things to make her happy.

Her sisters lay in bed all morning and then sat around
complaining, while Beauty was up with the birds to welcome
her father downstairs with a cheery,

"Fried mushrooms for breakfast! I found a real treasure trove
of them in the wood."

"You are my treasure now, Beauty," he would say, with tears
in his sad old eyes.

They lived like this for a year. Then, one day, a messenger rode to the cottage and told the merchant that one of his ships had turned up. It had not been wrecked, after all, but had taken shelter in a far-off country, and had now finally arrived back at the port, filled with goods.

"I must go down to the coast and sort things out," said the merchant. "Now, what will I bring you back?"

"New dresses – at last!" said the elder sisters. "And face cream, and silk stockings, and precious gems, and perfume, and hats with feathers on them and . . ."

"What about you, Beauty?" asked her father. "You haven't asked for anything yet."

"I would like a rose," said Beauty at once. "A beautiful pink rose."

The merchant was away for a long time, but at last he set out for home, loaded down with presents for his daughters. He had found everything on their list except for a rose, and it was now winter so nothing was growing except thorn bushes.

The merchant was not far from home, when suddenly a great snowstorm blew up and swirled round him. The snow was so thick that his horse could hardly see where it was going.

The merchant rode along, the snow settling thickly on his hat. He hoped he would soon find a house where he could seek shelter. In the distance he could hear hungry wolves howling, which made him anxious, and he urged his horse on.

At last, just when he thought he could go no farther, the merchant saw a light shining dimly through the snowflakes and he rode toward it. He was amazed to find that the light was pouring out of the windows of a splendid palace.

The merchant knocked on the door, but no one answered. His horse was tired out, so he put it in the empty stables, where he found fresh water and oats waiting. Then the merchant trudged back through the deep snow to the palace, and pushed the heavy door which creaked slowly open.

"Hello?" called the merchant, but there was no answer, so he walked through the hall into a large room with a roaring fire. There was a wonderful smell of roast chicken, and he saw a table, set for one with gold plates and knives and forks.

The merchant took off his wet coat and hat and wandered over to the table, where a large roast chicken glistened in the firelight.

"I'm sure whoever lives here won't mind if I sit down," he thought.

So he sat at the table and waited. And waited.

When the gold clock on the wall struck eleven, the merchant could stand it no longer. He grabbed the roast chicken, which was still hot and moist, and tore it into pieces and began eating. He had never tasted anything as good. There were plates of roast potatoes, crispy onion rings, and peas that tasted as if they were just out of the garden, even though it was winter.

When he had washed all the food down with some good red wine, the merchant noticed a silver bowl of strawberries and cream on the table.

"I could have sworn that wasn't there a moment ago," he said to himself, before he ate them. The strawberries were the reddest and ripest he had ever eaten, and tasted delicious.

By now the merchant was feeling very sleepy. He set out to explore the palace, making his way through many grand rooms. At last he came to a room with a fire glowing in the fireplace and a canopy bed with the covers turned down. Without thinking, the merchant took off his clothes and slipped between the sheets, which were crisply laundered and smelled of lavender. At once he was fast asleep.

"Cock-a-doodle-do!"

The merchant woke with a start and sat up in bed. The sun was streaming into the room, and he jumped up and looked out of the window.

He rubbed his eyes. Was he still asleep and dreaming?

The merchant looked down on a garden that was in full, summer bloom. All the snow had vanished, and instead there were huge beds of roses, and grass as green as emeralds.

His old, travel-stained clothes had gone, and there was a new suit of clothes laid out in front of the fire. He washed with a jug of hot water that was steaming in front of a mirror, and dressed in the new clothes, which fitted him perfectly.

Back in the dining hall, the foods he liked best were heaped in silver dishes: juicy sausages, fluffy scrambled eggs, muffins that melted in his mouth and a pot of hot chocolate.

He ate his fill, and stood up to leave.

"Whoever you are, thank you!" he shouted before he went off to saddle up his horse.

The merchant was leading his horse out through the beautiful garden, when he remembered his promise to bring back a rose for Beauty.

"The garden is full of roses," he said to himself, "and the owner of the house has been so generous, he will not miss just one."

So the merchant stopped and picked the largest, pinkest rose he could see.

At once there was a huge roar, and a beast appeared in front of him. It was so horrible to look at that the merchant almost fainted.

"So this is the thanks I get!" roared the beast, "I give you shelter from the storm, I feed you and lay out new clothes, and what do you do?"

The merchant trembled.

"You steal the things I love most – my roses. Well, for that you will die."

"I . . . I only wanted one rose as a present for the thing I love most – my daughter, Beauty," stammered the merchant. "Is there nothing I can do to save my life?"

"Nothing," roared the beast, "unless, that is, you promise to return, bringing with you the first thing that greets you when you get home."

When he heard that, the merchant smiled with relief. He had a little black dog that was always first to run out to meet him when he came home after a long journey.

So he agreed, put the rose carefully in his hat, and quickly set off home.

Beauty was shaking a quilt out of a bedroom window in the cottage, when she saw her father riding in the distance, with the rose in his hat bobbing up and down.

"I don't believe it – he's found a pink rose!"; she cried, and she rushed out of the cottage and ran down to the front door to meet him. The little black dog, meanwhile, was dozing in front of the fire.

"My dear daughter," said her father to Beauty. "I have paid a dreadful price for this rose." And he told her how he had promised to send the beast the first thing that met him.

"Don't worry, Father," said Beauty, "I will gladly go. The beast can't be as bad as you say, and perhaps he will let me come home if I ask him kindly."

The next day, Beauty and her father were both red-eyed and tired, because neither of them had slept a wink.

"It's no good, you have to keep your promise," said Beauty, "But I'm sure it will work out for the best."

"Yes – off you go," said her sisters, who were busy trying on the fine dresses their father had brought home for them.

So Beauty and her father galloped off through the bare and chilly countryside. Both their horses seemed to know the way to the beast's castle, as if they had been there many times.

As soon as Beauty and her father rode into the palace grounds, they were surrounded by summer blooms and lush rose bushes.

"It's magic!" said Beauty, her eyes shining. "All these roses – in the middle of winter.

I can hardly believe it."

They tied up their horses and went inside the palace. In the dining hall, there were now two places set, and a delicious meal was waiting for them under silver covers.

"Come, Father," said Beauty bravely, "I will eat if you will."

They were just finishing large, ripe peaches that tasted of honey, when there was a terrifying roar outside the door, which grew louder and louder.

Beauty dropped her peach and stared at the door, which opened very slowly. There stood the beast – looking even more horrific than her father had described. He had put on his best clothes of a red velvet cloak and a white lace collar, but these only made him look even more ugly.

He sat down beside them at the table and said

"So this is the Beauty for whom you plucked my rose?"

"It is." said the merchant sadly, "she ran to meet me when I went home, but has insisted on coming back with me."

"I am glad that you did," said the beast to Beauty, and she was surprised to hear that his voice was soft and gentle.

"You must leave in the morning," said the beast to Beauty's father.

"Rest assured your daughter will be quite safe with me."

The next day, Beauty's father left her and rode sadly home. Beauty spent the day walking in the grounds among the sweet smelling roses.

After dinner, she was sitting in her room when there was a knock at the door.

"May I come in?" asked the beast.

"Of course," said Beauty, pulling another chair up to the fire.

The beast spoke so kindly to her, that when she looked into the flames, she quite forgot how ugly he was.

The next night, he came to her room again.

"Help yourself to the peaches and grapes that grow in my garden," he said, and his voice was kinder than ever.

On the third night, the beast brought Beauty a large bunch of pink roses.

"Oh, how lovely!" she gasped.

"Will you marry me?" asked the beast, sinking to his knees.

"I can't, my dear beast," replied Beauty.

"Then I will surely die," said the beast.

Two large tears rolled down the beast's ugly face, and he left the room.

Beauty soon discovered that the mirror in her room was magic. Sometimes she saw herself when she looked in it, and sometimes she saw a picture of other people and things that were happening somewhere else.

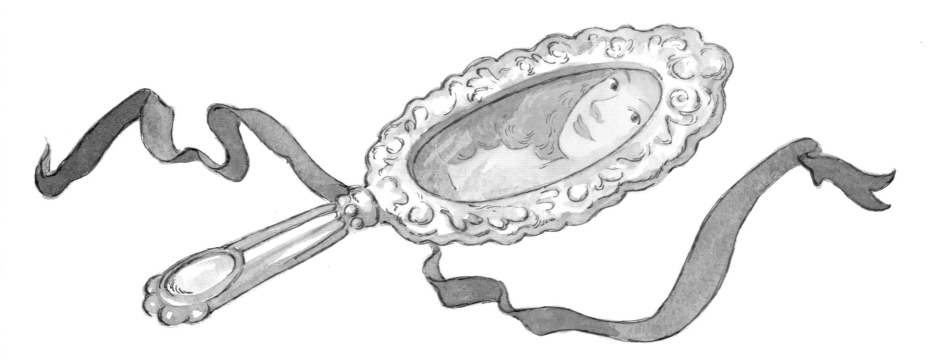

One day, she looked in the magic mirror and saw her poor father lying on his bed, looking very ill. She also saw her sisters in another room. They were happily curling each other's hair and laughing. They seemed to have quite forgotten their poor sick father.

When the beast came to her room that night, Beauty was very sad and told him what she had seen.

"I must go home and look after him," she said. "If I don't, he will surely die."

"And what about me?" asked the beast. But when Beauty began to cry, he agreed to let her go home for a week, as long as she promised to come back to him when the time was up.

The beast gave Beauty a special pink rose and said, "Hold this rose and wish, and it will take you wherever you choose. It will also bring you back to me, so don't forget your promise."

He left her, with a swish of his cloak, and Beauty at once wished herself back in her father's cottage.

She was just in time. Her father was very ill, but as soon as he saw Beauty he felt better. She made him a soup with special herbs that she had brought from the beast's garden, and he felt his strength come flooding back.

"Who does she think she is?" said her sisters crossly. "Fresh herbs at this time of year indeed, while we have to make do with old turnips!"

The sisters grew very jealous when Beauty described the beast's palace, with its wonderful rose garden and gold plates.

"I suppose our wooden bowls are not good enough for you now?" they jeered.

When the week was almost up, the sisters hatched a plan.

"Why should we have to slave away here, while she wanders about in her magic garden eating grapes? We'll stop her leaving, and then we'll see if her precious beast comes to get her," said one of the sisters.

"Oh, how exciting!" said the other.

So the two sisters pretended to be very fond of Beauty, and showered her with hugs and kisses.

"If you leave now, we're sure Father will become ill again," they said, and they went into the kitchen and sniffed onions to make themselves cry.

"We can't bear to think of you going back to that beast," they howled.

Beauty was so soft-hearted and kind that she agreed to stay for another week.

"Then I really must go back," she said, "because I promised."

She was rather surprised to find just how much she missed the beast, and their talks every evening by the fire.

At the end of the second week, Beauty kissed her father and told him not to worry.

"I am not frightened of the beast now," she said. "I know he would never do me any harm."

Her sisters were bored with waiting for the beast to come roaring up to the cottage, and didn't try to make Beauty stay any longer.

Beauty held the pink rose in her hand and wished herself back in her room in the beast's palace.

It was evening, and she waited for the beast to come, as usual, to talk to her, but he never came.

Beauty spent a sleepless night, tossing and turning, and in the morning she set out to look for the beast.

Beauty looked in all the rooms in the palace, but there was no sign of him, so she went out into the garden.

All the roses were covered in dew that sparkled with rainbows as she walked in her bare feet on the cool grass.

"Dear beast, where are you?" called Beauty.

At the very edge of the garden, where the grass changed into the winter countryside, Beauty saw the beast, lying on the ground.

"He is dead," she thought. "I broke my promise and I have killed him."

She knelt down, took his rough hairy hand, with its long claws, in her hands, and began to cry.

When her tears fell on his face, the beast opened his eyes and looked up at her.

"You forgot your promise to me, Beauty, and now I must die," he sighed.

"No," cried Beauty through her sobs, "What can I do to save you."

"Will you marry me?" asked the beast for the second time.

"I will," replied Beauty at once.

There was a bright flash of light, the beast vanished, and in front of Beauty stood a handsome prince.

"Where is my beast?" she asked, looking round.

"Here he is," laughed the prince, holding out his arms.

"A wicked witch put a spell on me, turning me into a beast until a beautiful girl agreed to marry me. You saw beneath my ugly disguise, and you have saved me."

The prince sent a gold carriage to fetch Beauty's father and sisters for the wedding.

So Beauty and her gentle prince were married, and, for the first time in years, the palace was filled with flowers and laughter.

After the wedding feast, Beauty's two sisters could be seen, scurrying around the garden bending over and carefully examining each rose bush.

"What on earth are they doing?" asked the prince.

"I think they are looking for a magic rose to wish for their own prince," said Beauty smiling, "but magic like this could surely only happen once in a lifetime."

A Storyteller Book

Sleeping Beauty

Many years ago, a king and queen lived in a large and magnificent white castle which had many tall towers and turrets.

The king and queen had almost everything they could wish for, but still they were not happy. The one thing they wished for the most, they could not have and that was a child of their own.

"How I wish we had a prince or princess to play hide and seek with among the apple trees," they sighed in the spring.

"Wouldn't it be lovely to have a child to build a snowman for?" they said in the winter.

One summer day the queen was soaking in her large silver bathtub which was beside an open window. Suddenly a green frog jumped in through the window and landed with a splash in her bath.

"Help!" screamed the queen. But the frog croaked, "Don't be frightened. Before a year is past, a princess will be born who will be as beautiful as I am ugly."

The frog was right. Soon the queen had a princess who was so beautiful that the king cried tears of joy and said,

"She was well worth waiting for."

The king decided to give a huge feast for all his family and friends, to celebrate the baby's birth.

"Don't forget to invite the fairies," said the queen. "You know that they can bring magic gifts, and they will bless our princess with luck and happiness."

There were thirteen fairies in the kingdom, but the king only had twelve gold plates. Everyone knew that fairies only ate off golden plates, so he only sent out twelve invitations. The thirteenth fairy was old and stooped, and the king thought she would be glad to rest at home.

"We will send her some cake after the feast," he said.

The day of the party came, and the palace cooks prepared a wonderful feast with heaps and heaps of chickens and hams and mountains of roast potatoes. The pastrychef baked a huge cake with pink icing.

After everyone had eaten, the fairies went up, one by one, to the princess's cradle to give her their presents.

"I give her the gift of laughter," said one, "so that she will never be sad for long."

"I give her the gift of a lovely voice," said another, "so that when she speaks, it will sound like music."

"I give her the gift of goodness," said a sensible-looking fairy, "so that she will not be loved for her beauty alone."

Eleven fairies had given their presents, and the king and queen were glowing with pride, when suddenly the doors of the banquet hall flew open and everyone gasped.

Suddenly, into the room hobbled the oldest fairy, dressed in a black cloak, and shuffling along with the help of a cane.

"So you didn't bother to ask me?" she cackled bitterly, "Well, I came anyway. And of course I too have brought the princess a magic gift."

Then, the oldest fairy hobbled over to the cradle and pointed a long bony finger down at the baby.

"When you are sixteen," she cursed, "you will prick your finger on a spindle and fall down dead!"

Then she turned, and before anyone could speak, she was gone from the room.

All the guests were speechless with shock, and the queen burst into tears.

Everyone had forgotten the twelfth fairy. She had not yet made her gift, and now she stepped forward.

"I can't wipe out another fairy's magic spell," she said, and the queen sobbed more loudly, "but I can help a little. The princess will prick her finger on a spindle, but instead of dying, she will fall into a deep sleep that will last for a hundred years."

The king did everything he could to try and escape the curse on his beloved daughter. He made a law that all spindles were banned from his kingdom, and they were all gathered up and thrown on a huge bonfire.

Posters were stuck everywhere warning that anyone found with a spindle would spend the rest of their days locked in the deepest dungeon in the king's castle.

The princess grew up to be beautiful, happy and good, and the king and queen tried to forget about the terrible curse.

On the princess's sixteenth birthday, everyone was busy preparing for her party.

She looked into the ballroom, and the maids screeched, "Go away! We're decorating the walls!"

She went into the greenhouse and the gardeners shouted, "Go away, the flowers are supposed to be a surprise!"

The princess loved running down to the kitchen for a slice of bread warm from the oven, with honey. The servants were always glad to see her, because she was kind to everyone, but today they said,

"Go away! For heaven's sake, you might have seen your birthday cake!"

Everywhere the princess went, people said, "Go away. It's a surprise!"

The king and queen had driven off in their carriage to fetch a small, golden puppy they were going to give her. At last, the princess was so bored, that she decided to explore some parts of the castle where she had never been.

She looked in dusty rooms and along hallways with creaky floorboards. Suddenly she came to a narrow, winding staircase that she had never seen before.

"I wonder where that leads," she thought. She climbed the stairs, and cobwebs brushed against her golden hair.

At the top of the stairs was a thick, wooden door, and from behind it came singing and a strange, whirring noise.

The princess pushed open the door and went in. A little old woman was sitting at a spinning wheel, singing and holding something pink and fluffy. Her spindle moved as fast as the wind, its point catching the light from the window.

"What are you doing?" asked the princess.

"I'm spinning some fine pink silk," said the woman.

"Oh, how clever!" said the princess, watching the spindle going back and forwards. "What a clever machine. Can I try?"

She reached out her hand. As soon as she touched the spindle, she pricked her finger and fell down on to the pile of silk, in a deep, deep sleep.

The sleep spread all over the castle like molasses. The king and queen, who had just come home, fell asleep in the castle hall. The puppy they had brought for the princess fell asleep with its head under its front paws.

The men and women of the court fell asleep where they sat, their drinks at their elbows.

The wind dropped, and the flags on the turrets stopped fluttering. It was as if the whole castle held its breath.

A thick hedge of sharp thorns began to grow all around the castle walls.

Every year it grew some more, until the whole castle was hidden, even to the tip of its highest flag pole.

One bright morning, a handsome young prince came riding into the kingdom.

"Where is the magic castle with the beautiful princess?" he asked. "My grandfather has told me all about her, and I am here to rescue her."

Everyone laughed at him. "We have heard that story, too," they said. "There have been other princes who have come here. They have tried to cut their way through the hedge, but they have all been trapped in the thorns and left to die."

One of the good fairies heard that the prince had arrived in the kingdom, and was asking everyone where the castle was.

She was very worried, because the hundred years would not be over until the next day. She knew that if the prince tried to cut his way through the hedge he, too, would be trapped in the sharp thorns.

So, the good fairy thought of a plan that would slow down the prince's journey, and also let her know if he was as good as he was handsome.

The prince was riding along a road when he came upon an old man trying to cut down a tree. He was huffing and puffing and could hardly swing his axe.

The prince got off his horse and tied it to a tree.

"Can I be of help, old man?" he called, striding over.

"My fire has gone out and I am too old and weak to cut any wood," said the old man, who was really the fairy in disguise.

"Stand aside!" said the prince, and he took the axe and cut down the tree. Then he chopped it into firewood and stacked it outside the old man's cottage.

"Thank you," said the old man. "Good luck will follow your kindness."

"I hope so," said the prince. "I am looking for the castle with the sleeping princess," and he rode on his way.

Next, the fairy turned herself into a cat and jumped down to the bottom of an empty well.

The prince was riding along, when he suddenly felt so tired that he got off his horse and sat down to rest beside the well. He took some bread and cheese out of his saddlebag, and had just begun to eat when he heard a faint, mewing noise. He looked all around but could see nothing.

At last he traced the sound to the old well. Looking over the rim, he saw a black and white cat, looking very sorry for itself, at the bottom of the well.

"If I leave it there, it will surely starve to death," he said.

The prince looked around for some rope, but could see none.

In the field beside him, there grew some long, tough grass. The prince cut a good bunch with his sword, and braided them into a rope. Then he tied the rope to the end of his horse's tail and backed the horse up to the edge of the well. He dropped the rope down until it reached the bottom and called down,

"Grab onto the grass with your claws, little cat, and hold on tight. We'll soon have you out."

The cat gripped the grass rope, the prince led the horse forward from the well, and the cat was pulled up.

"There we are," he said, setting it free.

The cat purred, and the prince could almost have sworn that it said, "Good luck."

The prince rode on. There was still no sign of the hedge of thorns, and he could see no one to ask. Suddenly, in front of him on the road, he saw an old woman, struggling with a huge and heavy bundle.

"Can I help you?" called down the prince from his horse.

"I have to get my bundle home before nightfall," said the old woman, "but it seems to be growing heavier at every step."

"Do you live near here?" asked the prince.

"I live at the very end of that path, in the middle of nowhere," she said, pointing down the dusty lane.

It was surely out of the prince's way, but he said, "Come up behind me on my good horse, and I will speed you home."

He reached down and helped her up. Then he hoisted the bundle up in front of him and set forth, and at every stride the horse took, the weight of the old woman and the bundle seemed to grow lighter and lighter. At last they reached her old, rundown cottage, just as night was falling.

"I am looking for the hedge of thorns, and the castle with the beautiful, sleeping princess," explained the prince as he helped the old woman dismount from his horse.

"Stay here tonight," said the old woman. "You can't travel in the dark. I'm afraid I can only give you a mattress on the floor and some stew."

The prince was not proud, and stayed the night. He was surprised to find that the stew was the best food he had ever tasted, and the mattress felt as soft as a feather bed.

In the morning, the old woman, who was, of course, the fairy, thanked him.

"Turn right at the end of the path," she told him. "Good luck will follow your kindness."

The prince did as she said, and there, right in front of him, rose the thick hedge of thorns.

"How strange," he thought. "I'm sure I would have noticed this yesterday."

At that very moment, the hundred years had just finished. He rode on his horse to the hedge of thorns and as he trotted up, it burst into blossom before his very eyes. A path opened up in the hedge and he was able to ride through, the blossom waving all around him. At last he had found the castle.

The prince got off his horse and marched up to the castle. In the yard, he saw horses sleeping standing up and cats curled up like fat, soft cushions. In the hall he found the king and queen, fast asleep on the floor beside the puppy. He explored some more and found all the men and women of the court slumped in their chairs, fast asleep.

He clattered, in his silver spurs, down to the kitchens. There was the cook fast asleep with her mouth open and the kitchen boy sleeping with a worried look on his face.

A kitchen maid was sitting, sound asleep, holding a chicken that was half plucked.

The prince looked in all the bedrooms but, of course, they were empty because it was morning when the sleep had crept over the entire castle.

"I will search every corner until I find the princess!" he said, and his voice echoed from the silent, stone walls – the first sound in a hundred years.

At last the prince found the winding staircase that led to the highest turret. He climbed it and pushed open the creaky, heavy door. Inside lay the princess, as beautiful as ever, with a slight smile on her lips as if she were dreaming. The prince, who had never seen anything as lovely, did not stop to think. He kneeled down beside her and kissed her gently.

At the touch of his lips, the princess woke up, stretched her arms above her head, and smiled at him.

"I've had such a lovely long sleep," she said, "I wouldn't be surprised if it was nearly dinner time. Shall we go and see?"

The prince and princess went downstairs hand in hand, and found the king and queen waking up. The puppy woke up and began to bark. The people at court woke up and finished their drinks. The cook woke up and scolded the kitchen boy. The fire leapt up again and the meat turned on its spit. The kitchen maid woke up and continued plucking the chicken.

Out in the yard the horses woke up and shook their manes. The grooms woke up and the cats woke and stretched. The flies crawled up the walls and the spiders scurried in corners.

The princess led the prince down to meet her parents.

"Happy birthday!" they said to her.

The princess held out the prince's hand. "I have had the loveliest dream," she said, "and look at the wonderful birthday present I woke up to find!"

The castle door opened, and there stood the old woman the prince had helped the day before.

"What are you doing here?" he asked.

At that moment, the old woman changed back into the good fairy and said,

"The hundred years are up. The spell is broken!"

The king and queen gasped with joy and when the prince asked if he could marry their daughter, they agreed at once.

"Instead of a birthday party, we will have a wedding!" they said happily.

As word spread throughout the castle that the spell was broken, everyone began to dance wildly with one another and cheer.

But the prince looked into the princess's lovely eyes and said joyfully,

"For us, the magic is only just beginning."

Aladdin

A long time ago, in China, there lived a boy called Aladdin.
His father had died and he and his mother were very poor.
They lived in a very small house near the edge of the town, and
his mother made a little money by washing and ironing huge
piles of laundry.

"Where are you, Aladdin? Come and help me wring out these
towels," shouted his mother, looking out the kitchen door. But
Aladdin was off wandering in the countryside, as usual. He
loved to walk in the fields and dream up all sorts of new plans
for becoming rich.

Suddenly a stranger appeared and began patting Aladdin on the back. He could not recall having seen the man before, which wasn't surprising because he was really a wicked magician in disguise.

"Aladdin, don't you recognize your old Uncle Ebenezer?"

"I've just come home from my travels abroad and I'm really glad I've bumped into you, because I need your help."

He took Aladdin's arm and marched him through the fields until they came to a grassy bank with a stone slab in its side.

"There's a cave behind here," went on the magician. "I would love to climb inside myself, but I'm afraid I'm too fat. But you could slip in like an eel. There's an old oil lamp in there I want. It looks ordinary, but I'm rather attached to it."

Then the magician warned, "But beware, you must not touch anything else you see in the cave!"

Aladdin was curious to see what the cave looked like. He was always hoping an adventure would turn up. Perhaps this was one. So he held his breath and wriggled through the narrow opening and down a few rough stone steps into a large cave.

A dim light shone down from the opening above, and it took Aladdin's eyes some time to get used to the gloom. But when they did, they grew wider and wider. On all sides were piles of gold, silver and jewels. In the corner was a gold statue with a diamond necklace and a silver crown. In its hand was a dull old oil lamp, looking out of place among the sparkling riches.

Despite the magician's warning, Aladdin could not resist stuffing necklaces and gold coins into his pockets.

'Mother will never have to wash even a hankie again,' he smiled to himself.

"Have you found the lamp?" boomed a loud voice.

Aladdin had forgotten all about the magician.

"I'm coming," he called back, trying to slip more gold coins into his shoes.

"Hurry up!" shouted the magician. "I'm warning you, I won't wait much longer."

Aladdin fetched the old oil lamp and shuffled over to the stairs. But he was so weighted down with gold and jewels that he couldn't wriggle back out.

"I can't leave all this behind," he wailed. "Uncle, I don't know what to do."

"I'll tell you what you can do," screamed the magician, who was tired of waiting, "you can stay there forever!"

There was a thud and everything went black. Aladdin was trapped inside.

'What good are all these riches if I never get out of this dark cave?' he thought.

He began to feel his way round the cave. He felt the foot of the statue, and beside it the old oil lamp which he had dropped when the slab slammed shut. 'I wonder why uncle wanted this old thing, when he could have had all these jewels,' he said to himself, as he sat down clutching the lamp.

It was nearly dinner time, and when Aladdin thought of his mother putting a bowl of tasty rice and fish on the table, a tear fell on the lamp. Without thinking, he rubbed it away with his sleeve.

FLASH!

There was a huge bang and the cave was lit up by bright lights, like fireworks, making the gold and jewels dazzle. Then a wisp of white smoke curled out of the spout of the oil lamp. Aladdin pressed himself against the cave wall, as first a face and then an enormous body appeared in the air above him.

"At last! I thought I was stuck in there for another hundred years!" boomed a loud voice.

Then the huge man with polished brown skin swung his long pigtail around as he noticed Aladdin. At once he bowed to him, golden hoops glittering in his ears: "The Genie of the lamp, Master, at your service. I have been waiting for a hundred years for someone to rub the lamp and let me out."

"Now, what is your wish?"

'This is probably all a dream,' thought Aladdin.

"I would like to go home, to my mother, please." he said.

There was another flash, and instantly Aladdin found himself in his mother's kitchen, still clutching the lamp.

Aladdin's mother was about to scold him for being late, but when he pulled the gold and diamonds out of his pockets, she fell back on a pile of newly-ironed sheets and gasped.

"But that's not the best thing," said Aladdin, "Our troubles are over – we can have whatever we want, thanks to the Genie of the lamp." His mother didn't believe him, so he rubbed the lamp and the Genie appeared.

"Send all the washing back, and fetch us a banquet with roast duck," commanded Aladdin.

Then a table set with mouth-watering dishes arrived in front of them and his mother had to believe him.

"When we've had enough to eat," said Aladdin, "we'll ask the Genie to build us a fine house to live in."

Soon they were happily settled in their new large white villa.

Not long afterwards, Aladdin was walking through the market when the crowd scattered to let a gold carriage through.

Looking inside as the carriage flew past, Aladdin saw a girl with long black hair and eyes like violets. She was even more beautiful than all his new treasures.

"Who is she?" he asked a stall holder.

"That's Jasmine, the Sultan's daughter," said the man.

"She is the girl I will marry," declared Aladdin.

The stall holder roared with laughter and said, "You don't understand. Her father will only allow her to marry a prince."

Aladdin spent the rest of the day thinking about Jasmine. When night fell, he got down the old oil lamp and rubbed it. With a flash, the Genie uncurled himself from the spout and hovered over Aladdin.

"What is your wish, Master?"

"The Sultan's daughter, Jasmine . . ."

"Ha!" laughed the Genie, "I wondered how long it would be before collecting more jewels became boring!"

"Jasmine," went on Aladdin, "I would like to meet her."

"Certainly, Master. Go up on to the roof and wait."

Aladdin went up onto the flat roof of his house and looked up at the stars. He thought about Jasmine's eyes, until he heard a swishing noise like the wings of a huge bird.

He was amazed to see a carpet flying through the night sky, with Jasmine sitting on it. It floated just above the roof and Aladdin helped her down.

"I was walking in the palace garden," said Jasmine, "when the carpet whisked me off my feet and brought me here. It must be magic!"

"Not as magic as the light in your eyes," said Aladdin. "Will you marry me?"

"I am lonely," said the princess, "and I can see that life with you would be exciting, but my father, the Sultan, says that I may only marry a prince."

"But I am a prince," said Aladdin. "I have a palace outside the city that is even grander than your father's."

"I don't believe you," laughed the princess.

Aladdin sent her home on the carpet. "I will call for you soon," he said as he waved her off.

As soon as Jasmine was gone, Aladdin rubbed the old oil lamp and the Genie appeared.

"Build me a palace that is even grander than the Sultan's."

"With pink marble domes and fountains?" asked the Genie with a yawn.

"Oh yes! And peacocks on the ground, because their tail feathers are like huge, beautiful eyes."

So Aladdin and his mother went to live in the grand palace. As soon as they had moved in, Aladdin invited the Sultan and his daughter to visit.

"Why have we never met before?" asked the Sultan.

"Because I have been searching the world for the most beautiful girl to be my princess," said Aladdin, taking Jasmine's hand, "and now I have found her."

The Sultan was dazzled by Aladdin's wonderful palace and the feast that the Genie had prepared for them. This must be a very rich prince indeed!

When his daughter asked to be allowed to marry Aladdin, he readily agreed.

Aladdin and Jasmine were married and rode home to their own palace in an open carriage. When they rode through the market, people threw flowers into the carriage for luck.

The wicked magician, who had been abroad, was amazed to see Aladdin sitting in the carriage beside the princess.

"Ah," thought the magician, "I must pay the happy couple a visit." He gave a horrible laugh and went off into the crowd.

A few days later, Aladdin decided to take his mother for a drive in their fine new carriage, while Jasmine picked some flowers. She was putting them in a vase, when she heard a voice outside calling, "New lamps for old!"

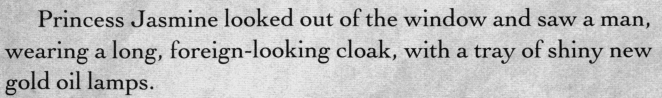

Princess Jasmine looked out of the window and saw a man, wearing a long, foreign-looking cloak, with a tray of shiny new gold oil lamps.

"I could give him that dirty old oil lamp of Aladdin's," she said to herself. "I've always thought it was strange that he's kept it. It looks so out of place among our gold dishes. Aladdin will be so pleased when he comes home and finds that I've got a lovely shiny new one."

She rushed out to the man and gave him Aladdin's old lamp.

"Here is your lovely new lamp," said the lamp seller.

The princess took it, and went back inside the palace.

At once the lamp seller, who was the wicked magician in disguise, rubbed the lamp and the Genie appeared with a great flash of light.

"What is your wish, Master?"

"Take this palace, and the princess, to the other side of the world!" roared the magician.

When Aladdin came home, he found a huge hole in the ground where his palace had stood.

Where was his palace, and his beautiful wife?

"The Genie will get them back," he said to himself. Then, with a thud in his stomach like the slab slamming shut on the cave, he remembered that the lamp was inside the palace!

"I will find Jasmine again," he vowed. "I won't stop until I find her, even if she's on the other side of the world."

Aladdin set out to look for his princess, living on scraps of food and sleeping under the stars. His gold coat became tattered and his feet grew hard and blistered with walking.

At last, after many years, when he had almost crossed the whole world, Aladdin saw the pink marble domes of his palace, shining in the distance through the morning mist.

"At last!" he said. "Now I must find my way back into the palace, and into my princess's heart."

Aladdin crept to the back door and stole inside. Along one of the corridors he found a beautiful girl scrubbing the floor.

"Aladdin!" she whispered. "You have come at last!"

He looked more closely, and saw that it was Jasmine, dressed in rags, but still with the same huge violet eyes.

"The magician is living in our palace," she sobbed, "and he keeps me as his slave."

"Where is the old oil lamp?" whispered Aladdin.

"He keeps it beside him at all times," said Jasmine.

"Does he ever have a nap?" asked Aladdin.

"Every night, after dinner, in front of the fire," said Jasmine.

"Then let's wait till then," said Aladdin. "We have waited so long, a few more hours won't hurt."

So Jasmine cooked an extra large dinner, and soon the magician was snoring gently in his chair. Aladdin tiptoed into the room and Jasmine pointed to the lamp, which lay on the floor beside the magician.

Aladdin took the lamp and rubbed it. There was a huge flash and the Genie appeared and hung just below the ceiling.

Jasmine jumped, and clung on to Aladdin. The magician woke up and tried to grab the lamp, but the Genie pointed a finger at him, and he stayed rooted to his chair, trembling with anger and fear.

"Master," boomed the Genie, rolling his eyes down at Aladdin. "What is your wish?"

"Fly my princess and me, and our palace, back home to China," said Aladdin.

They felt the ground beneath them lift, as if a tree was being torn up by the roots.

The pink palace flew through the air and landed with a soft thud back in China.

"Now what shall we do with the wicked magician?" asked Aladdin.

"Have you any ideas?" he asked the Genie, who was just about to get back into the lamp.

"The worst thing that I can think of," said the huge Genie, and his voice was quiet for once, "is to be shut up in that old oil lamp for a hundred years, until someone finds it and rubs it."

To Aladdin's horror, tears rolled down his fat cheeks.

"I hadn't thought of that," said Aladdin.

The magician was trembling with fear, and pressing himself against the palace wall.

"You wouldn't d-do it," he stammered. "Just think – you would have no more wishes!"

"I don't need a Genie to grant wishes now that I have found Jasmine again," said Aladdin. "I have everything I want."

Aladdin turned to the Genie.

"I wish that you would put the magician in the oil lamp and bury it back in the cave, where it can stay for another hundred years."

The Genie pointed a finger at the magician, who began a loud wail which grew fainter and fainter as he shrank smaller and smaller and disappeared down the spout of the lamp.

The lamp went hurtling out of the window, on its way to the cave in the hillside.

The Genie was sobbing quietly. "Free at last!" he gulped. "The magician has taken my place. How can I ever thank you?"

"Wish us luck," said Aladdin. "We will never be able to thank you enough."

"Before you go," he added, "I do have one last wish."

The Genie looked worried, because his magic powers had gone with the lamp.

"I'm afraid I can't produce any more riches or banquets," he sighed. "Not even one gold coin! Not even one giant shrimp!"

"My wish," said Aladdin, "is that Jasmine and I will live happily ever after."

A huge grin spread over the Genie's face.

"Your wish is granted," he beamed.

"I am sure you will live happily ever after."

And they did!

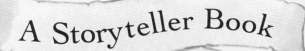

Peter Pan

It was bed time in the nursery, but John, Wendy and Michael didn't feel at all tired. Their parents, Mr and Mrs Darling, were going out to dinner.

"Take care of the children, Nana," said Mrs Darling.

"Woof!" barked the large dog who lived in the nursery and looked after them. She had just filled the bath and tested the water with her paw.

"You go first, Michael, you're the youngest," said Wendy.

"I don't want a bath," said Michael, but Nana scooped him up and carried him off on her back, howling.

When Mrs Darling came back into the nursery to say goodnight, she heard a strange noise at the window. She rushed over, just in time to see the shape of a small boy, trying to open it. But when she opened the window and looked outside, there was no one there.

"I think I know what he's looking for," she said. The day before, Nana had seen a boy at the window, and she had bounded over and shut it so fast that she had cut off his shadow. Mrs Darling had folded it and put it away.

Mr Darling was in a bad mood because Nana had rubbed against his black trousers, and left long dog hairs all over them. And now Michael was refusing to take his cough medicine.

"Why doesn't Daddy take some of the medicine to keep Michael company?" suggested Wendy. Two doses were poured out but, while Michael drank his, Mr Darling poured his into Nana's bowl. Nana plodded over and drank it, thinking it was a treat. What a face she made!

"Oh, poor Nana!" said all the children, and they made such a fuss of her that Mr Darling said crossly, "The proper place for dogs is outside." He took her out and chained her up in the yard.

Mrs Darling tucked the children up in bed and tiptoed out of the room. In the quiet, dark nursery the children yawned, stretched and soon fell sound asleep.

Suddenly a tiny ball of fire darted into the room, zig-zagged round it, and disappeared into a jug. There was a click at the window. It flew open and a boy stepped inside and walked round the room as if he was looking for something.

At last he said. "Tink, do you know where they've put it?" The ball of fire flew over and rested on a drawer of a chest, making a tinkling noise. The boy ran over, opened the drawer, and pulled out his shadow.

"Oh well done, Tinker Bell! What a clever fairy you are," he shouted. "But how am I going to stick it on again?"

He fetched a bar of soap that Nana had left behind, and rubbed it all over his feet. Then he soaped his shadow and tried to stick it on to his feet, but it wouldn't stick.

"I will never have a shadow again," wailed the boy, and he burst into tears.

He sobbed so loudly that Wendy woke up, sat up and said,
   "Why are you crying?"
   The boy jumped to his feet and asked. "Who are you?"
   "Wendy Darling. Who are you?"
   "Peter Pan," said the boy.
   "Where do you live?"
   "I live in Never-Never Land." He pointed to the dark
window. "It's second turning to the right, and straight on till
morning."

"What a funny address," said Wendy, "but you know you'll never stick your shadow on like that. I'll sew it on for you."

She jumped out of bed and fetched a needle and thread and Peter let her sew it on. It stung quite badly when the needle went in and out, but it was worth it. Soon he was dancing up and down the nursery, watching his shadow make patterns on the floor as he threw his arms and legs about.

"How old are you, Peter?" asked Wendy.

"I don't know," he said, "because I ran away from home when I was very, very young. I heard my parents talking about what I would do when I was grown up. And I don't ever want to be grown up," he added, stamping his foot and making his shadow jump.

Suddenly there was a tinkling noise from the chest drawer. Peter pulled it open and Tinker Bell flew out.

"Oh!" cried Wendy, "Is that a fairy?"

"Of course it's a fairy," said Peter matter-of-factly. "And don't say you don't believe in them, because every time some silly child says that, a fairy dies."

"Do you live alone, Peter?" asked Wendy, watching Tinker Bell flit round the room.

"No, I live with the Lost Boys. They all fell out of their prams when their mothers were looking the other way."

Wendy gasped and put her hands up to her mouth, but Peter went on, "It's not so bad – if they are not claimed within seven days, they are sent off to Never-Never Land. I am their Captain."

"It sounds like fun," said Wendy, "but what made you come to our nursery window?"

"I often come, to hear your mother telling you all bedtime stories. The Lost Boys have no mothers to tell them stories, so I go back and tell them yours. And I must go back now. They'll wonder where I am."

"Oh, please stay," begged Wendy.

"I've got a better idea," said Peter, "why don't you come with me? Then you can tell us all stories and tuck us in at night."

"But I can't fly," said Wendy.

"I can teach you."

"And John and Michael, too?"

"Of course."

John and Michael were shaken gently awake, and told about Never-Never Land. "There are Indians there," said Peter, "and mermaids in the lagoon and, of course, the pirates . . ."

"Did you say pirates?" asked Michael, rubbing his eyes.

"Yes," said Peter, "we're always having to fight them."

"Let's go," shouted John, punching his pillow.

They tried to fly around the nursery, flapping their arms behind Peter, but they couldn't get off the ground.

"Wait while I sprinkle some fairy dust on you," said Peter. "Now wiggle your shoulders like this." Suddenly they could all fly as easily as birds.

"Now, Tink, lead the way," said Peter, standing on the window sill. She shot ahead like a star, and Peter held Wendy's hand as they all floated out into the night sky.

A moment later, Mrs Darling, who had just come home, rushed into the nursery, with Nana at her heels. But they were too late. The beds were empty. The children were already on their way to Never-Never Land.

The Lost Boys were wondering where Peter was. Slightly Soiled, the eldest, was playing a tin whistle and dancing with an ostrich, while Tootles, Nibs, Curly and the Twins looked on. They wore fur skins, because it was winter, so they looked more like bears than boys.

"Sh! Listen!" whispered Nibs suddenly. It was their enemies, the pirates. The boys just had time to scuttle down the stairs they had made in hollow trees, to their home in a secret underground cave.

"Yo ho, yo ho!" sang Captain Hook, the pirate chief, as his men pulled him along on a sledge. He waved his right arm in time to the music. Instead of a hand, it ended in a shiny hook – which is where he got his name. Peter Pan had cut off his hand in a fight and thrown it to a crocodile. The crocodile liked the taste so much that, ever since, it had wandered over land and sea, licking its lips as it searched for the rest of Captain Hook.

Luckily for the pirate chief, the crocodile had swallowed an alarm clock, and he always knew when it was coming. Every tick-tock sent shivers from his head, with its long, greasy black curls, right down to his toes.

"I'll rest here!" shouted the Captain, hauling himself on to a huge mushroom. "I'm on fire!" he roared suddenly as he felt his seat getting hotter and hotter. When he leapt up, he found that he had been sitting on the chimney of the Lost Boys' home, which Peter Pan had disguised with the mushroom.

"Ha! Ha! I've got them, now!" cackled Hook. But then he thought he heard a ticking noise. He took to his heels and ran into the forest, with his fat first mate, Smee, puffing along behind him.

The Lost Boys clambered out of their tree trunks again.

"Look at that huge white bird," said Nibs, pointing at Wendy, flying overhead in her nightgown. Tinker Bell was jealous because Peter liked Wendy so much, and she shouted down to Tootles to shoot her. He aimed with his bow and arrow, shot up into the sky, and Wendy fell to the ground.

"It's not a bird – it's a girl!" cried the boys in horror, as Peter Pan flew down to join them.

"I'm all right," whispered Wendy. "The arrow hit a button."

"We won't move you," said Peter. "You rest there and we'll build your own Wendy house around you."

They made the house out of wood from the forest, and put John's top hat on the roof as a chimney. When it was finished, they all piled inside. There was even a fire in a grate, and the light flickered on a row of happy faces as Wendy told them the first bedtime story that was all their own.

When summer came, Peter took the children down to the lagoon, where the mermaids lived.

"There's one!" shouted John, pointing. She was sitting on a rock, combing her long hair. John managed to catch hold of her tail, but she wriggled away like an eel.

The children had all climbed on to the big rock, when they saw the pirate ship sailing towards them.

"Look!" said Peter. "They've got Tiger Lily – the chief of our friends, the Indians."

Over the years, Peter had learned to speak exactly like Captain Hook. "Let her go, lads!" he bellowed, in Hook's voice. So the pirates cut Tiger Lily loose. She jumped overboard and swam towards Peter.

"You fools," shouted Hook, "I'll capture her myself." He rowed over and jumped on to the rock.

"Quick! Row Tiger Lily to the shore," said Peter and sprang at the pirate chief. The boys took her off in Hook's rowing boat while Wendy watched Peter and Hook fighting fiercely on the slippery rock. At last Hook was exhausted, and had to swim back to the pirate ship.

Wendy was stranded on the rock, too tired to swim to shore, and the tide was rising fast. Suddenly a large kite came flying over the lagoon. Peter was able to reach up and catch its tail, and tie it round Wendy.

"Good luck," he shouted as she soared off towards land.

The water was already lapping Peter's feet, when a sea bird came floating past on its nest, which had been blown off the cliff by the winds.

"Just in time," cried Peter, as he shooed the bird off and leapt in. He held out his jacket to catch the wind, and sailed to shore.

One night, Wendy told the boys a story about a mother and father whose children flew away to Never-Never Land. "But they always kept the nursery window open, in case they came flying back one night," she finished.

"It's not like that," said Peter, sadly. "I went back to my nursery window, but the window was barred and there was another little boy sleeping in my bed."

"What if there are other children in our beds?" said Wendy in horror. "We'd better go home at once."

"Don't go," begged the Lost Boys.

"You can all come, too" said Wendy. "I'm sure Mother would love to keep you all." They were very excited then, and rushed off to pack their baby clothes.

"I shan't come," said Peter, "because then I would have to grow up."

"Well, always remember to take your medicine, when we're gone . . ." began Wendy, when suddenly they all heard loud clashings overhead.

"The pirates and the Indians are fighting," said Nibs.

At last the noise stopped. The Indians had been beaten, and had run off.

Hook bent down and listened at the mushroom chimney.

"If the Indians have won," he heard Peter say, "they'll beat the tom-tom."

"Aha!" said Hook, and he picked up a tom-tom the Indians had dropped and began to beat it.

"You're safe now," said Peter, not realising that they were being tricked. "Tink will show you the way."

So one by one, the children crept up the tree trunk stairs. Then the pirates pounced and carried them off to the pirate ship.

Hook himself lay in wait for Peter, but he never appeared.

"Well, he shan't escape," said Hook. "I heard the little mother tell him to take his medicine? A good idea!" He stretched his long arm down the chimney, poured poison into Peter's glass, and stole away.

Peter was feeling very lonely and sad, when Tinker Bell flew into the cave. "The pirates have got them!" she said.

Peter leapt up and grabbed his sword, and, as he stopped to take his medicine before he left, brave Tinker Bell flew into his glass and drank it. "It's poisoned," she said, in a weak voice. Her light began to grow very faint.

Peter stood in the middle of the cave and shouted, "Would all the children who believe in fairies clap their hands!" A thunderous noise of clapping echoed round the cave, Tinker Bell's light grew strong again, and she set off with Peter to rescue Wendy and the boys.

On the pirate ship, Hook lounged in a deckchair and bellowed, "Bring up the prisoners!" The boys appeared, followed by Wendy in a long cloak.

"Tie her to the mast," shouted the pirate chief, pointing his hook at Wendy.

"Now, which of you boys wants to be first to walk the plank? Don't be shy!" said Hook with a crooked smile. Just at that moment, there was a loud tick-tock.

"Quick!" screamed Hook, "Hide me! It's the crocodile!"

The sailors clustered round him, with their backs to the deck, so none of them saw Peter Pan climbing over the ship's side. In his hand was a ticking alarm clock. Peter tiptoed into the cabin.

When the ticking stopped, Hook said, "Right. Shall we start with you?" and prodded John with his hook.

At that moment that was a loud, wailing noise from the cabin.

"We're h-haunted," stammered Hook, beginning to tremble.

"Send the children in," he said.

The children were pushed into the cabin beside Peter, and the noises grew louder until the pirates crowded together and shook with fear and screwed up their eyes. None of them saw the children creep out and hide on deck.

Peter untied Wendy and secretly took her place, hidden beneath her cloak.

"Get rid of the girl," shouted a pirate. "Everyone knows that girls bring bad luck on a ship."

"No one can save you, now," said Hook, shaking his hook at the figure in the cloak. Peter Pan threw back the hood and cried, "Wrong again, Hook!"

The pirates gasped as the children rushed out from their hiding places, armed with weapons from the cabin.

"They must be ghosts," shouted fat Smee. "Whatever was making that awful noise has killed them." The pirates threw themselves overboard in terror, and Peter Pan and Hook were left facing each other on the deck.

"This time, we fight to the finish," said Peter, waving his sword above his head.

Hook was driven right to the edge of the deck.

"You'll never beat me," shouted Peter above the wind, "because I will always be young and strong."

He knocked Hook's sword away and pushed him over the side. Down below, the crocodile was waiting. It opened its mouth as if it was giving a huge yawn, and Hook fell right into its smiling jaws.

Back at home, the children's father and mother were sad and
lonely.

"If I hadn't taken Nana out of the nursery, this would never
have happened," said Mr Darling.

To punish himself, he decided to live in the dog's kennel until
the children came home. He was carried to work in it and, when
he came home, it was taken up to the nursery where Mrs
Darling spent most of her time.

One evening, as Mrs Darling was sitting beside the fire in the nursery, she fell asleep. While she slept, three small figures flew in through the window and landed with soft thuds in their beds.

"Mother," called Wendy.

Mrs Darling woke with a start. So often she had dreamed that the children had come home. But this time, when she looked over, there were bumps under the quilts. Then the children threw back the covers and ran over to her.

"You've come home. At last!" she shouted, trying to put her arms round them all at once.

Mr Darling heard the noise and came rushing in, with Nana bounding behind him, barking joyfully.

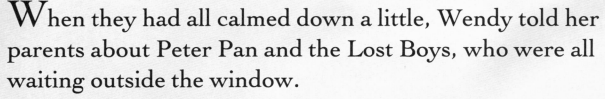

When they had all calmed down a little, Wendy told her parents about Peter Pan and the Lost Boys, who were all waiting outside the window.

"You mean those poor children have no mothers?" said Mrs Darling. "Well, of course, they must come and live with us."

They all came in and sat beside the fire, as if they were waiting for a story.

"Will you stay, too, Peter?"

"I can't," he said, moving towards the window, "It would mean growing up. But I will miss you all."

"Why don't I fly to Never-Never Land every year, in the spring," said Wendy, "to make sure you're all right?"

"Then I'll keep the little house we made for you," laughed Peter happily.

"I'll put it up in the trees."

"But will you remember the way, Wendy?"

"Of course."

Peter Pan jumped on to the window sill, ready to fly, as Wendy
and all the boys chanted together, "Second turning to the right,
and straight on till morning."

Peter Pan flew back to Never Never Land,
the land where children never grow up; and as
far as we know, he is there still.

A
Storyteller Book

Red Riding Hood

There was once a little girl who lived on the edge of a forest with her mother and father. She loved to play outside among the trees even when it was cold and frosty, so her mother made her a bright red cloak with a hood to keep her warm. But her daughter liked it so much that she wore it all year round, and soon she became known as Red Riding Hood.

One day her mother said to her,

"Your grandmother is ill, so I want you to go and visit her and cheer her up. I have made some cakes and put them in this basket. Stop on the way at the dairy for fresh butter, at the miller's for fresh bread, and at the farmyard for fresh eggs."

Red Riding Hood's mother handed her daughter the basket.

"Now, off you go but remember," she warned, "watch out for wolves. They are crafty creatures and are not to be trusted."

Red Riding Hood put the basket over her arm and set off. She had not gone very far, when a hungry wolf, padding through the forest, stopped and sniffed the air.

"I smell fresh cakes," he said to himself. Then he sniffed the air again.

"Even better," the wolf thought gleefully, "I smell a lovely fresh tasty child."

He slunk silently through the trees until he saw Red Riding Hood's cloak glowing in the distance.

The wolf tucked his tail between his legs, and padded softly over the ground, after her.

Red Riding Hood skipped along until she came to the dairy.

"Hello?" she called out.

There was no answer. Where was the dairymaid?

Red Riding Hood went into the cool milk shed where the cows stood in a row, swishing their tails.

There was still no sign of the dairymaid, so she walked around the back of the dairy into the fresh green field where the cows liked to graze.

"Oh!" gasped Red Riding Hood excitedly when she saw what was there.

A light brown cow was standing beside the dairymaid, and they were both looking down at a tiny, new-born calf.

"How sweet!" said Red Riding Hood.

"Sweet it may be," said the dairymaid, wiping her brow with her freckled arm, "but it was a real surprise. This calf wasn't expected for a couple of weeks – and now it's been born out in the field instead of in a barn with soft straw. I can't leave it here – it's beginning to get cold already – and all the cows are waiting to be milked."

At once, Red Riding Hood took off her cloak and put it over the calf, who looked up at her with huge brown eyes.

"Can you stay here while I run and fetch a wheelbarrow lined with straw?" asked the dairymaid.

When she came back, the dairymaid lifted the calf gently into the barrow and wheeled it off to the barn, its mother following behind, mooing.

Red Riding Hood put her cloak back on, and was about to go on her way, when suddenly she remembered why she had stopped at the dairy.

"The butter!" she cried, "I almost forgot. May I have some fresh butter for my grandmother, as she's not well?"

"Of course," said the dairymaid, taking a chunk out of a barrel and shaping it quickly into a block.

"Take this as a thank-you for lending your lovely red cloak. The calf was just beginning to shiver when you arrived."

Red Riding Hood put the butter in her basket, and skipped on her way.

The wolf saw her red hood, bobbing up and down in the distance, and zig-zagged quietly through the trees, after her.

Soon Red Riding Hood saw the sails of the mill turning around in the wind up ahead, and she ran up the path.

Usually the miller came out to greet her, but there was no sign of him.

Red Riding Hood pushed open the heavy wooden door, and looked inside. The miller was sitting on a stool, his head in his hands, staring at the white, dusty floor.

"What is the matter?" asked Red Riding Hood.

"You'll never believe this," he answered sadly, shaking his head so that a cloud of flour flew into the air, "but I've run out of sacks. I sent out a big order of flour this morning, and my new sacks haven't arrived yet. That means I can't carry the flour down to the oven and bake a batch of loaves for my special customers – like you."

"It also means," he added glumly, "no bread for my supper."

Red Riding Hood took off her cloak and held it out to him.

"Pile the flour onto my cloak and we'll carry it to the kitchen together."

The miller leaped to his feet and rushed off to the mound of flour which had collected at the bottom of a chute. He scooped it on to the cloak, and he and Red Riding Hood carried it carefully, between them, down to the kitchen.

The oven was hot and ready, so, the miller quickly mixed and kneaded some dough and shaped it into loaves. Then he sprinkled them with flour and put them in the oven.

"Time for a rest and a drink," he smiled, and poured out two glasses of cool lemonade.

Soon a wonderful yeasty smell filled the kitchen. The miller opened the oven, and took out the loaves with his long, flat wooden paddle.

"We'll give your red cloak a good shake outside," said the miller.

"Thank you," said Red Riding Hood. "Oh, and I almost forgot, may I have a loaf of bread for my grandmother. I'm on my way to visit her because she is ill."

"Of course," said the miller, and he chose the largest, flouriest warm loaf and put it in her basket.

"I don't know what I would have done without your red cloak," he said, waving to her at the gate.

Red Riding Hood skipped on her way, and the wolf pricked up his ears as twigs snapped under her feet.

"Ah, there she is, I thought I'd lost her," he said to himself, and he quietly got up and crept after her.

Red Riding Hood ran along until she reached the farmyard. The wolf slunk back when she went through the gate. The farmer had a big gun, and he would love to shoot the wolf, who had eaten many of his chickens in the past.

"Oh no!" growled the wolf. "Missed her again. But I can wait."

Meanwhile, Red Riding Hood looked all round the farmyard. Where was the farmer?

At last she found him, standing at the edge of the duck pond, scratching his head.

"What's the matter?" asked Red Riding Hood.

"It's that silly duck," said the farmer, pointing to the middle of the pond.

"It's got its foot stuck in some weeds, and it can't move. The water is too deep for me to wade out, and I don't know what will happen when it gets dark."

Red Riding Hood looked around the yard until she saw the lid of a large wooden box used for packing eggs. She pushed it onto the water, sat on it, and held out her red cloak like a sail.

The wind caught her cloak, and it ballooned out behind her, sending her speeding across the pond until she reached the duck. She managed to untangle its foot, and it was so tired that it let her lift it on to the lid and sail back to the bank.

"Bless my soul!" said the farmer, helping her onto dry land and taking the duck from her.

He put the duck gently on the ground, and it waddled off, quacking loudly.

"Come inside and have something to eat," said the farmer.

"I can't," said Red Riding Hood, "I'm on my way to visit my grandmother, who's ill."

"And that reminds me, may I have some new-laid eggs for her?" she asked.

"It's the least I can do," said the farmer, and he packed half a dozen large ones among some straw in her basket.

"Thank you. Goodbye!" called Red Riding Hood, and she skipped on her way.

The wolf watched Red Riding Hood leave the farmyard. He came out from his hiding place and raced around ahead of her. Then he sauntered back until he met her coming the other way.

"What a lovely day!" he said, smiling and licking his lips, "And where are you off to, my dear?"

He was so friendly that Red Riding Hood forgot all about her mother's warning to watch out for wolves.

"I'm off to visit my grandmother, who lives in the cottage on the other side of the forest," she answered.

The wolf thought quickly. Perhaps he could manage to have a larger meal than the one he had planned. A two-course one!

"How lucky your grandmother is to have such a pretty visitor," smiled the wolf.

"Does she like visitors?"

"Oh she loves them," said Red Riding Hood, "because she lives all alone."

"Does she really?" said the wolf, showing his large white teeth in a grin,

"Well I'm sure she'll have a lovely surprise. Goodbye and good luck."

The wolf waved his paw.

"Mother was quite wrong," said Red Riding Hood to herself as she skipped on her way, "I think wolves are very charming, handsome animals . . ."

She stopped at a clearing in the middle of the forest to pick some flowers for her grandmother.

"Just one more," she said as she picked each one, running from clump to clump, until a whole hour had passed and she had gathered a huge bunch.

"Grandmother will love these," she thought, and she skipped happily on her way.

The wolf, however, didn't waste any time. He raced between the trees and arrived very quickly at the cottage on the other side of the forest.

He knocked on the door and an old, frail voice called out, "Who's there?"

"It's me, dear Grandmother," replied the wolf in a small high voice.

"Red Riding Hood, who else?"

"I'm in bed, but the door's open, my dear, so just push it and come in."

The wolf pushed open the door and his bright eyes darted round the room until he saw the bed, with Red Riding Hood's grandmother propped up on the pillows, a white lacy nightcap on her head.

The wolf hadn't eaten for two days and his mouth watered. The old woman didn't even have time to scream. He bounded over to the bed and gobbled Grandmother up so quickly that she slipped down his throat before she knew what was happening!

The wolf put on her nightcap and leaped in between the bedcovers, making sure his tail was tucked well out of sight. Then he snuggled down in the warm bed and waited.

Soon there was a knock at the door.

"Who's there?" called the wolf, making his voice sound as much like the poor old woman he had swallowed as he could.

"It's me, Grandmother, Red Riding Hood. I've come to cheer you up, and I've brought you some cakes, some butter, some new bread and some fresh eggs. Oh – and also a huge bunch of flowers, because I know how much you love them."

"Not only that, continued Red Riding Hood but I've had lots of adventures on my way here, and I'll tell you all about them."

"That sounds so exciting," croaked the crafty wolf, "come in, my dear."

"I can tell by your voice that you've got a bad cold," said Red Riding Hood, coming into the cottage.

"That's right, my precious," said the wolf hoarsely, "better stay back a bit in case you catch it."

Red Riding Hood looked over to the bed, where the wolf's face was peeping over the edge of the blankets.

"You don't look like yourself at all today, Grandmother," said Red Riding Hood. "I think I got here just in time."

"I think so, too" said the wolf, trying hard not to burp. He had swallowed the old woman so fast that he was suffering from dreadful rumblings and pains in his stomach.

"Grandmother!" said Red Riding Hood, "How big and shiny your eyes seem today!"

"All the better to see you with, dear one," croaked the wolf.

"And how long and pointed your nose looks all of a sudden."

"All the better to smell you with," snarled the wolf softly, licking his lips.

"And your ears," went on Red Riding Hood, "seem to be sticking straight up like antennae."

"All the better to hear you with," smiled the wolf, wiggling them from side to side.

"As for your teeth," said Red Riding Hood, backing away slightly, "they're absolutely enormous!"

"All the better to eat you with!" roared the wolf, bounding from the bed and swallowing her down in one huge gulp!

After such a large two-course meal, the wolf felt very full and sleepy, so he climbed back into bed and was soon fast asleep and snoring as loudly as a foghorn. A woodcutter was passing by when he was stopped in his tracks by the noise.

"I knew the old woman in that cottage was ill," he said to himself, "but if she's making that much noise, she must be really bad. I'd better drop in and see how she is."

He pushed open the door and saw the wolf, his head lolling against the pillow in its nightcap and his mouth wide open and snoring loudly.

The woodcutter saw at once what had happened. He rushed forward, threw back the bedcovers and before the wolf knew what was happening, the woodcutter had slit open the wolf's stomach with his axe.

Red Riding Hood jumped out, followed by her grandmother, blinking in the light.

"Oh, thank you," she cried, "it was horrible in there and so dark and damp."

The woodcutter filled the wolf's stomach with large stones and the old woman sewed it up with her strongest darning thread.

Then the woodcutter and Red Riding Hood carried the wolf to the lake behind the cottage and threw him in. There were a few bubbles and he sank without trace.

Back inside the cottage, Red Riding Hood's grandmother had a
fire going and was putting some water on to boil.

"I feel so much better," she said, "I think the shock of being
inside the wolf's stomach has cured me. Now, I hope you can
both stay for supper."

"At last," laughed Red Riding Hood, "now I can taste the cakes, the bread, the butter and the eggs, and tell you the story of what happened on my way here."

"I think I've had enough excitement for one day," said her grandmother, spreading butter on some bread.

"Quite right," boomed the woodcutter in his deep voice, stroking the polished axe on his knee.

"When you've eaten, Red Riding Hood, I will take you home through the forest."

"I think you'll find that word of what's happened will spread through the forest as quick as lightning, and you'll never ever again be troubled by a big bad wolf."

And he was right.

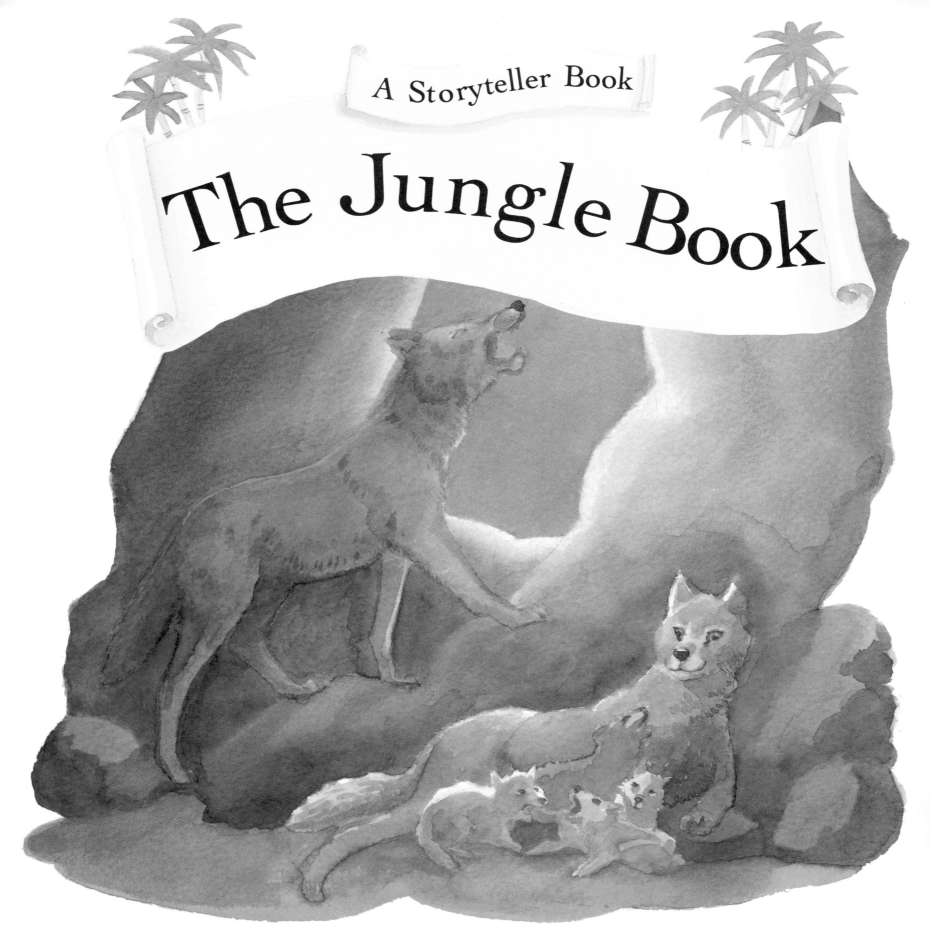

The Jungle Book

In a cave deep in the Indian jungle, a grey wolf woke up from his day's rest, yawned and stretched himself. The moon shone in at the mouth of the cave, where Mother Wolf was lying, while their four cubs jumped all over her, squealing.

"Time to hunt again," said Father Wolf. He was just about to go out hunting when he was stopped in his tracks by a loud angry snarl, coming from far below in the valley.

"That's Shere Khan, the tiger," said Father Wolf to his wife. "He hasn't caught anything, and now he's frightening off my prey for tonight as well!"

"Wait. Listen," said his wife. Shere Khan's voice had changed into a humming purr that filled the heavy jungle air.

"He's not hunting bulls or bucks tonight," she went on, "That's the sound he makes when he's hunting man."

The noise grew louder, and ended in the deafening roar of the tiger charging, followed quickly by a painful howl.

"I know what's happened," said Father Wolf, "the stupid beast has jumped on a wood-cutter's camp fire, and burned his feet."

"Quiet! Something is coming up the hill," said Mother Wolf, twitching her ears.

Father Wolf went outside the cave and got ready to spring at the rustling bushes. He bounded high into the air, but suddenly saw what he was leaping at, and stopped himself just in time, landing with a soft thud back down in the same place.

"Look!" he cried, "A man-cub!"

Right in front of the cave, was a small brown boy, just old enough to walk. He looked up into the wolf's face and laughed, showing white teeth and dimples.

"I have never seen a man-cub," said Mother Wolf, "bring it here." Father Wolf's jaws closed over the boy's back, and he carried him into the cave as gently as if he were carrying an egg. He dropped the man-cub amongst his own litter, and immediately the boy was pushing the wolf cubs aside, to get to their mother's warm fur.

Suddenly the moonlight was blocked out of the cave as Shere Khan's huge head appeared just inside.

"My prey – a man-cub – came this way," roared the tiger. "Its parents have run off, and now I want it. Give it to me."

The wolves knew that Shere Khan could not squeeze into the narrow cave.

"The wolves are a free people," growled Father Wolf. "We take orders from the head of the pack, not from you."

The tiger's roar filled the cave with a noise like thunder, and the cubs sprang back in fright, but Mother Wolf patted the boy with her paw and snarled fearlessly at the tiger.

"The man-cub is mine! He will learn to live with the pack and hunt with the pack, and in the end he will hunt YOU too Shere Khan!"

The tiger knew better than to fight an angry mother and he backed out of the cave. As he slunk back downhill, he roared over his shoulder,

"The man-cub will end up between my teeth sooner or later."

"Will you really keep him?" asked Father Wolf, when Shere Khan had gone.

"He came here alone, naked and hungry, but he was not afraid," said Mother Wolf.

"Of course I will keep him. I will call him Mowgli, little frog, but we will have to take him to the next pack meeting."

On the night of the pack meeting, Akela, the big grey lone wolf who led the pack, lay stretched out on a huge rock. Below him in a circle sat about forty wolves of every size and shade.

Suddenly Mowgli was pushed into the middle of the circle by Father Wolf. He sat there, laughing and playing with some pebbles in the moonlight. Akela was looking down at him, and all the wolves waited to hear what he would say, when the muffled roar of Shere Khan came from behind the rocks:

"The cub is mine. Give him to me. What use have you for a man-cub?"

The law of the jungle laid down that, in order to join the wolf pack, a cub must be spoken for by at least two members of the pack who were not his mother and father.

"Who speaks for this cub?" barked Akela.

The only other creature allowed at the pack council was Baloo, a sleepy brown bear who taught the wolf cubs the law of the jungle. He got up on his hindquarters and growled,

"I will speak for the man-cub. Let him run with the pack, and I will teach him."

"We need one other voice," said Akela.

A dark shadow dropped down into the circle. It was Bagheera, the black panther, who was as cunning as a fox but had a voice as soft as wild honey.

"I know I have no right to be here," he purred, "but I will give you a bull I have just killed if you will accept the man-cub into the pack. It would be a shame to kill a cub as smooth and naked as that one – and it may be more fun to hunt it when it is grown."

The voices of lots of wolves rose in the night air:

"It will scorch in the summer sun, anyway. What harm can a naked frog do us?"

"Take him away," said Akela to Father Wolf, "and train him as a free pack member."

So Mowgli went home with his new wolf family, laughing all the way, and never guessing how close to danger he had come.

During the next ten summers Baloo taught Mowgli the law of the jungle. He showed him how to tell a rotten branch from a good one, and many other things.

"Speak politely to the wild bees, when you come across a hive," he told him, "and they might give you some honey."

"And always warn the water snakes before you splash down into one of their pools," he added.

One day, Bagheera, the black panther, was lying in the shade, watching Baloo teaching Mowgli.

"How can his little head carry all these things?" Bagheera asked the big bear.

"Is there anything in the jungle too little to be killed?" answered Baloo. "That's why he must learn."

Mowgli ran over and jumped on to Bagheera's back, pulling at his fur and chattering loudly,

"Don't worry, Bagheera. Some day soon I'm going to have a tribe of my own and lead them through the branches. And then we'll throw twigs and dirt down on old Baloo!"

"Wait a minute," said Baloo, scooping Mowgli off the panther's back with his huge paw, "you've been talking to the monkeys, those silly creatures who eat everything and don't have any laws."

"I was tired of learning all these rules," said Mowgli, "so I went off on my own and the monkeys came down from the trees and played with me."

"We jungle creatures don't have anything to do with the monkeys," said Baloo, as a shower of nuts and twigs rained down on their heads.

The monkeys were always meaning to get a leader, and have laws of their own. They never did because they couldn't remember anything from one day to the next. But they were very angry when they heard Baloo call them silly animals, not fit for Mowgli to play with.

"I've had an idea," screeched one monkey. "Let's capture the man-cub. He can show us how to build shelters – I've seen him weave sticks. We could make him our leader and all the other animals would be jealous."

The monkeys followed Baloo, Bagheera and Mowgli through the jungle very quietly until it was time for their midday nap. Mowgli, who had promised to have nothing more to do with the monkeys, was sleeping soundly between the black panther and the bear. The next thing he knew, Mowgli was being pulled along by lots of strong, hard little hands. He looked back and saw Baloo, up on his hind legs, giving a huge roar and waking up the whole jungle.

The monkeys dragged Mowgli up a tree until he felt the thin, topmost branches bending beneath him. Then the monkeys, holding him tightly, flung themselves into mid-air and caught hold of the branches of the next tree with a great *Whoop*!

The monkeys were going so fast that Mowgli knew his friends would soon be left far behind. If he looked down, all he saw was a thick sea of branches. So he looked up, and there he saw Chil the hawk, balancing and wheeling on the wind as he flew over the jungle looking for prey.

Chil was amazed to see a man-cub being rushed through the trees by the monkeys. But he was even more amazed when the little brown figure shouted up a perfect hawk call, just as Baloo had taught him.

"Mark my trail and tell Baloo and Bagheera where I am," called Mowgli.

Meanwhile, Baloo and Bagheera were panting after the monkeys. Every now and then, Bagheera climbed up a tree, but the thin branches would not bear his weight and he slithered back down, his claws full of bark.

At last he stopped and said, "What we need is a rescue plan. They may drop him if we follow too closely."

"You're right," said Baloo, "I know – we must find Kaa the rock snake. The monkeys are terrified of him because he can climb as well as they can, and he steals young monkeys in the night. The very mention of his name makes their tails go cold."

Baloo and Bagheera found Kaa stretched out on a warm ledge admiring his beautiful new coat. For the past ten days he had been out of action, changing his skin, and now he was feeling splendid and looking forward to dinner.

"Good hunting!" called Baloo.

"He!" hissed Kaa. "Don't speak to me about hunting. The branches are all dry and rotten, so I have to spend half a night climbing on the chance of catching one young monkey."

"Don't speak to me about monkeys."

"Yes, monkeys are so rude," said Bagheera. "To call a noble creature like yourself a footless, yellow earth worm . . ."

Kaa hissed again and the muscles in his throat tensed in anger.

"They called me thissss?"

Just then Chil the hawk swooped down and called to Baloo,

"I have a message for you from the man-cub. The monkeys have taken him to the monkey city."

"So, Mowgli remembered the hawk call even while he was being dragged through the trees," said Baloo proudly.

The three animals sped off to the monkey city. It was called the Cold Lairs, and was an old deserted city, built by man, but now buried deep in the jungle where few animals, apart from the monkeys, ever went.

In the Cold Lairs, the monkeys were very pleased with themselves and their new plaything. Mowgli looked around in amazement at the grand, crumbling buildings all covered with ivy. There was a great palace without a roof, and trees were growing through its walls.

"I'm hungry," said Mowgli at last. "Bring me food or let me hunt here – it is the law of the jungle."

Some monkeys bounded away to fetch him nuts and papayas, but they started squabbling together and completely forgot what they had set out to do.

Mowgli could do nothing but wait.

Bagheera reached the Cold Lairs first. The black panther paced up the slope and ran like a dark streak through the rows of monkeys, striking them with his paws.

"Hide the man-cub!" screeched a crowd of monkeys, grabbing Mowgli and dragging him towards an old summer house. They stood on each others' shoulders to make a pyramid pulled Mowgli up and pushed him in through the broken roof.

Mowgli fell as Baloo had taught him, and although it was a long way down, he landed on his feet and was not hurt. From high up above, Mowgli could hear yells and scufflings. For the first time since he was born, Bagheera was fighting for his life.

"Go to the water tank, Bagheera," shouted Mowgli, "the monkeys can't swim."

Mowgli's cry gave Bagheera new strength, and he began to work his way through the mass of monkeys to the water tank. Suddenly a war cry rang out through the air. Baloo had arrived. He began to move through the monkeys, clearing a path with wide swipes of his paw.

Mowgli heard a huge splash, which told him that the panther had found the water, where the monkeys could not follow. But there were so many of them. Where was Kaa, the snake?

Bagheera lifted up his dripping chin and gave a snake call. Kaa had been slithering along as fast as he could, but he had only just reached the Cold Lairs. He raised his head and held his body up like a battering ram as he struck into the crowd of monkeys around Baloo.

"It's Kaa! Run for it!" screamed the monkeys when they saw him. They knew that one tight squeeze from Kaa's long body was enough to kill a monkey, and they all scattered in terror. Everything went quiet, and then Mowgli heard Bagheera shaking the water from his fur.

"I'm in here," shouted Mowgli, and his friends followed the sound of his voice to the old summer house. Kaa looked until he saw a crack in the walls. Then he lifted his long body up clear of the ground, and struck six blows at the bricks. The walls broke and fell away in a cloud of dust, and Mowgli leapt out and flung himself between Baloo and Bagheera, putting an arm round each neck. Kaa looked him up and down.

"Be careful," hissed the snake, "that I don't mistake you for a monkey, some dark night when I have just changed my skin."

The moon was now sinking behind the hills, and all the monkeys had gathered again and were huddled together along the old ruined walls.

Kaa coiled his body into a circle, swinging his head from side to side. Then he began making loops and figures of eight with his body, and humming a low, lazy song. Bagheera and Baloo were rooted to the spot. The monkeys swayed forward helplessly, and Bagheera and Baloo took another step forward with them.

At once Mowgli put his hands firmly on the bear and the panther, and the two animals jumped, as if they had been awakened from a dream.

"Keep your hand there," mumbled Bagheera, "or else I will have to go back to Kaa."

"Don't be silly," laughed Mowgli, "it's only old Kaa making circles in the dust."

The man-cub, the panther and the bear slipped out through a gap in the wall and back into the jungle.

When Mowgli had been in the jungle about ten years, Bagheera the panther said to him,

"Akela is very old and some day soon he will no longer be the leader of the pack. Many of the young wolves believe Shere Khan when he says that a man-cub has no place in a wolf pack."

"I was born in the jungle!" exclaimed Mowgli. "There is no wolf from whose paws I have not pulled a thorn."

"If you feel under my chin," purred Bagheera, "you will find a bald spot, rubbed by a collar. You see I, too, was born among men, and lived in a king's palace until I escaped. That's why I gave a bull for you at the pack council when you were just a tiny cub. Now you must go back to men or you will be killed in the jungle."

Bagheera looked kindly at young Mowgli,

"I think you are in danger already, but you can run down to the huts in the valley and take some of the red flower that the people there grow. That will be a stronger friend to you than either Baloo or me."

The red flower was fire. The animals all feared it so much, that they could not even call it by its proper name.

Mowgli ran down to the valley and pressed his face against the window of a hut. He saw a boy picking up a pot, which he filled with lumps of red-hot charcoal and took outside.

Mowgli strode over, took the pot from the boy and rushed off with it, leaving the boy howling with fear.

Mowgli blew into the pot and dropped twigs into it to keep the fire going as he carried it back up the hill.

That night, at the council meeting, Shere Khan the tiger began to speak.

"What right has he to speak," shouted Mowgli, "just because Akela is growing old? Tigers do not belong in our pack."

Shere Khan roared angrily,

"This man-cub was meant to be my dinner from the start. He has troubled the jungle for ten seasons, but what has a man to do with us?"

"A man! What has he to do with us?" yelled more than half the wolf pack.

Mowgli stood up and shouted at them, "I, the man, have brought a little of the red flower which you, dogs, fear."

He threw the pot of fire on the ground amongst some dead wood and the pack drew back in terror before the leaping flames. Mowgli picked up a branch, lit it in the flames and beat Shere Khan over the head with it until the tiger whimpered with fear.

"Go, singed jungle cat," shouted Mowgli, "and the next time I come to this rock it will be as a man – with your hide. "GO!"

Soon there was no-one left at the council rock except Mowgli, Akela, Bagheera and a few wolves. Suddenly something made Mowgli catch his breath, and hot tears ran down his cheeks.

"What are these?" he said, wiping his face, "Am I dying, Bagheera?"

"No, little brother," said the panther sadly, "but now I know you are a man, and not a cub. The jungle is no longer a safe home for you. They are only tears Mowgli, let them fall."

"I will go to men now," said Mowgli, "but first I must say goodbye to my mother."

Mowgli went up the hill to her cave, and cried on her soft coat.

"Come back soon and see us, little frog," said Mother Wolf, "because I loved you more than any of my own cubs."

"Don't forget me," said Mowgli. "And tell everyone in the jungle – Baloo and all my friends – never to forget me."

Dawn was breaking and there were pink streaks in the sky when Mowgli strode down the hillside to meet the strange creatures called men.

Snow White

In the middle of winter, when the snow was falling as thickly as feathers, a queen sat at her window, sewing. She pushed open the black ebony window frame to see how deep the snow was. As she leaned forward, her needle pricked her finger and three drops of blood fell on to the snow on the window sill. It looked so pretty that the queen said, "I wish I could have a child with skin as white as snow, lips as red as blood and hair as black as ebony."

Soon afterwards, the queen had a daughter, and when she looked at her she saw that her wish had come true; the child had skin as white as snow, lips as red as blood and hair as black as ebony. "You will be called Snow White," said the queen, smiling down at the baby, and then she sighed and died.

After a while, the king married again. The new queen was very vain and couldn't bear to think that anyone was more beautiful than she was. She had brought with her a magic mirror which hung in her room in the palace, and she would often stand in front of it and ask,

"Mirror, mirror, hanging there,
Who in all the land's most fair?"
And the mirror would answer,
"O Queen, I always tell what's true,
The fairest in the land is you."

Meanwhile Snow White was growing up, and becoming more beautiful every year. One day, when the queen asked the mirror who was the fairest in the land, the mirror replied,

"Your beauty shines, as ever, bright,
But the fairest one is now Snow White."

When she heard this, the queen turned pale with rage. Every time she saw Snow White, she felt ill and trembled all over.

At last she could stand it no longer. She sent for the palace huntsman and told him, "Take Snow White into the deepest part of the forest and kill her."

When she saw the look of horror on his face, the wicked queen added, "And bring me back her heart, so that I know she is dead." The huntsman and Snow White walked until they came to the very heart of the forest, where the sun struggled to get through the trees. Snow White ran ahead, gathering a bunch of flowers, but she dropped them and screamed when the huntsman drew his knife and pointed it at her.

"It's no use," he cried, "The Queen wants me to kill you, but I can't do it. Run Snow White – run for your life."

Then the huntsman killed a young deer, cut out its heart and took it back to the wicked queen, whose eyes lit up when she saw it. At last I am rid of her," she said.

Deep in the forest, Snow White was running as fast as she could, with tears streaming down her face, so that she couldn't see where she was going. She bumped into trees and thorn bushes pulled at her clothes. Wild animals watched her rushing past, but none of them harmed her.

At last, as it began to grow dark, Snow White came upon a clearing in the forest with a cottage in it. She looked in through the window, but she could see no one.

"Perhaps I can rest here," she said to herself, pushing open the door and stepping inside.

There was a table spread with a thick white cloth. On it were seven small plates, with bread and cheese on them, seven knives and forks and seven mugs full to the brim with apple juice.

Against the wall were seven little beds with thick cotton quilts. "What tidy children!" said Snow White, "but where do the parents sleep?"

She was so hungry that she took a little bit of bread and cheese from each plate, washed down with a few drops of juice, and then she curled up on one of the small beds and fell asleep.

It was completely dark when seven lanterns bobbed up the path to the cottage. They were carried by seven dwarfs – little men who earned their living by digging in the mountains for gold. "What's this?" exclaimed the first dwarf when he had pushed open the door. "Our chairs are pulled out – and look, there's mud on the floor." "Look – crumbs!" said the second, pointing at the table. "Someone's been nibbling at our supper."

"Someone's been in here," said a third dwarf, scratching his long beard.

"What do you mean, 'been'?" whispered another of the little men, bending over one of the beds, "Who's this?" All the dwarfs clustered round, and one held a candle up to look at Snow White.

"It's a child – and look how beautiful she is!"

"Sh! Let her sleep," said the dwarf whose bed it was. "I will curl up on the hearth rug, and then if she wakes in the night and needs anything, I will be ready."

The dwarfs ate their supper as quietly as they could. Every night they had bread and cheese, because they had never learned to cook. They used to dream of stew and dumplings and strawberry shortcake.

Every now and then the dwarfs stopped eating and looked over at Snow White, sleeping peacefully, her face lit by the flickering candle.

After clearing away the supper things, the dwarfs washed, changed into their night shirts and climbed into bed.

"In the morning she will tell us her story and how she came to be here," they said.

Then they snuggled down and went to sleep, as excited as if it were Christmas Eve.

In the morning, Snow White sat up in bed and yawned, stretching her arms in the air. Then she rubbed her eyes. At the end of her bed were seven little men, all watching her.

"Oh!" she cried, "Where am I? And who are you?"

"Don't be frightened. We were wondering who you were," said one of the dwarfs, rushing off to fetch a tray with bread and butter and a mug of milk.

Between sips and bites, Snow White told them about her stepmother, the wicked queen.

"She wanted the huntsman to kill me," she said, and a tear dropped onto the tray, "but he wouldn't. I ran, and ran, and now here I am."

"And here you'll stay," said the dwarfs. "You can keep house for us while we go to work."

"Can I?" asked Snow White, cheering up. "Do you by any chance," she added, looking round at them all shyly, "like apple pie?"

The dwarfs began dancing with one another, shouting, "Hurrah! Apple pie for supper."

"Now, remember," they told Snow White when they left for work, their picks over their shoulders, "don't open the door to anyone. The queen will soon find out where you are and will come looking for you."

"I promise," said Snow White. "Now off you go. There will be a hot supper waiting for you tonight."

At the palace, the queen climbed the stairs to her room. Snow White was dead. The wicked queen went and stood in front of the magic mirror and asked,

"*Mirror, mirror, hanging there,*
Who in all the land's most fair?"

But the mirror answered,

"*With seven dwarfs in a cottage small,*
Lives Snow White – fairest of them all."

When she heard this, the queen knew that the huntsman had tricked her.

"He may have saved Snow White's life," she snarled, rushing from the room, "but not for long."

Down in the palace basement, the queen stirred some poison in a bowl until it bubbled and fizzed. She soaked a comb in the poison and put it in a basket together with some handkerchiefs and soap. Then she opened a trunk of old clothes and dressed herself in rags with a black cape over the top. She pulled on a gray, straggly wig and covered her face with thick make-up and a layer of white powder, until she looked like a poor, old woman.

Finally she put the basket over her arm, took a walking stick and hobbled out of the palace gates.

Snow White was busy making pie when she heard a voice calling outside: "Pretty goods for sale!"

'The dwarfs warned me not to let anyone in,' thought Snow White, looking out of the window, 'but this is only a poor old woman. What harm could she do me?' So she wiped her floury hands on her apron and opened the door to let her in.

"Is there anything here that catches your eye, my pretty one?" cackled the old woman.

The poison made the comb glisten with all the shades of the rainbow, and Snow White longed to pick it up.

"This comb would look lovely against your black hair," said the old woman. "Shall I put it on for you?"

"Yes, please," said Snow White. The wicked queen stuck the comb into Snow White's hair. At once Snow White fell down senseless at her feet.

"Ha!" laughed the queen. "Who's the fairest now?" and she threw down her walking stick and hurried back to the palace.

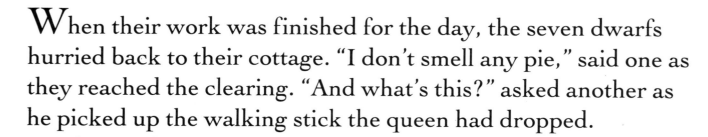

When their work was finished for the day, the seven dwarfs hurried back to their cottage. "I don't smell any pie," said one as they reached the clearing. "And what's this?" asked another as he picked up the walking stick the queen had dropped.

They rushed inside and found Snow White lying on the floor.

"She's dead," cried one, but when they picked her up to carry her to a bed, their lanterns shone on the poisoned comb.

"Look at that – quick, pull it out," said a dwarf.

So they pulled out the comb and soon Snow White was sitting up and telling them what had happened.

"That 'poor old woman' was the wicked queen," they said. "She is clever and she will disguise herself in lots of ways. Remember, you must not open the door to anyone."

At the palace, the queen threw off her rags, wiped her face clean, and went to her magic mirror.

"*Mirror, mirror, hanging there,*
Who in all the land's most fair?"

She just couldn't believe it when the mirror still gave the same answer as before:

"*With seven dwarfs in a cottage small,*
Lives Snow White – fairest of them all."

"Just wait," said the queen, "I can mix up a stronger poison."

Weeks passed and the dwarfs grew to love Snow White. They rushed home from their work in the mines, and as they reached the clearing they would sniff the smell of cooking in the air and shout out: "Chicken stew!" or "Apple dumplings!"

There was always a wonderful hot supper waiting for them, and flowers in a vase on the table. The shelves in the pantry were weighed down with cakes and pies.

"We never knew we were lonely until you arrived," they told Snow White. "Just think – seven of us and we were all lonely, but never again."

The queen had other plans. In the palace basement she was brewing up an even stronger poison. When it was ready, she took a green apple and dipped half of it in the poison. The half that was dipped came out a bright rosy red, so shiny that whoever saw it would long to sink their teeth into it.

This time, the queen disguised herself as a tramp, with a brown, weatherbeaten face and thick boots, and set off into the forest with a basket of apples.

"Ripe, rosy apples!" she called as she marched into the clearing where the dwarfs' cottage stood.

Snow White stuck her head out of the window. "I can't open this door to anyone. The dwarfs made me promise."

"Quite right too!" said the wicked queen. "What a sensible girl – here, let me give you an apple."

"No," said Snow White politely, "I promised not to take any presents."

"I suppose you're worried about poison," laughed the queen, "Look – I'll eat half of this apple, just to show you how safe it is."

She took a knife and cut the apple in half and took a big bite of the green side.

"There – I've saved the best half for you, my dear," she said, holding it out.

Snow White's mouth watered when she saw the shiny red apple. 'It must be all right if the tramp has eaten some herself,' she thought and she reached out and took it.

As she bit into it, Snow White noticed that the woman's finger nails were long and polished, not like a tramp's at all. But it was too late.

As soon as she bit the apple Snow White fell to the floor and lay there, dead.

The wicked queen laughed: "Let's see if the dwarfs can wake you up this time!"

When she asked the mirror that night who was the fairest in the land, the mirror answered,
    "O Queen, I always tell what's true,
    The fairest in the land is you."
    "At last!" shouted the queen.
    "At last I can have some peace!"

The dwarfs came home and found Snow White lying on the floor of their cottage, as white and as cold as snow.

They looked in her hair for a poisoned comb, but they found nothing – Snow White lay as if she were sleeping and having a lovely dream.

All the dwarfs sat round Snow White and wept. They had no heart for cleaning or cooking and the dust settled in drifts in their cottage.

After three days, they decided it was time to bury Snow White. "She looks so beautiful," sobbed one, "I can't bear to lay her in the dark earth."

"Let's make a coffin out of glass," said another," and then we can always look at her and remember how happy she made us."

So the dwarfs cut a coffin out of clear crystal and laid Snow White gently inside. They carried it to the top of a hill where the sun shone on it every morning, and one of them always sat beside it, watching over Snow White.

For many months Snow White lay in the glass coffin, looking as if she were not dead, but only sleeping.

One day, a prince was riding past and saw the sun shining on the crystal. He got off his horse and walked up the hill to see what it was. When the prince reached the top, he looked at Snow White, lying smiling inside and he thought that she was the loveliest thing he had ever seen.

"Let me have the coffin," he begged the dwarfs. "I will give you whatever you want for it."

"We would not part with it for all the gold in the mountains," said the dwarfs.

"Then let me have it as a present," said the prince. "I can't live without it, but I promise I will take great care of it always."

The dwarfs saw that the prince loved Snow White as much as they did. They finally agreed to let him take the coffin to a room in his castle. "You can visit her there whenever you want," said the prince.

"How I wish I had known her when she was alive."

The dwarfs were helping to carry the coffin down the hill, when they tripped and tumbled down the bumpy slope. The coffin jolted forward and the piece of poisoned apple fell out of Snow White's mouth. She yawned and stretched her arms, pushing up the lid of the coffin.

"Where are you taking me?" Snow White asked the dwarfs. "Is this a game?" Suddenly she saw the handsome prince, and she recognized him as the prince she had been dreaming about all the time she lay in the glass coffin.

"Oh, it's you!" she smiled, holding out her hand. He scooped her up and put her in front of him on his horse and they rode down the hill.

The dwarfs hugged one another and waved goodbye, tears of joy streaming down their faces.

"I will see you at the castle soon," called Snow White.

Snow White and the prince sent out invitations to their wedding to all of the great people in the land. However the prince himself rode to the cottage in the clearing to deliver invitations to the seven dwarfs.

"They are the most important guests," said Snow White.

The wicked queen heard that a grand wedding was planned.

"I hope the bride is not as beautiful as I am," she said, and went to her room to ask her magic mirror once more:

"Mirror, mirror, hanging there,
Who in all the land's most fair?"

To her horror, the mirror answered,

"You know I have to say what's right.
It is the new princess – Snow White."

The queen was so filled with hate and anger that she smashed the mirror with her fist. It shattered into a thousand pieces, and one of them pierced her heart. She was found lying dead among the broken glass.

Snow White and the prince were married in his castle in the mountains. The dwarfs watched proudly as she danced past in her white silk dress, and no one thought it was strange when they all threw their hats in the air and shouted, "Seven cheers for the prince and Snow White!"

The
End